MISTLETOE & NAUGHTY

A DARK NOEL NOVEL

KL HILL

e-Book AISN: B0FSX9TFF3

Paperback ISBN: 979-8-9923171-3-8

Cover design by The Red Fox Creative

Interior design and formatting by Sidebar Media, LLC

Editing by Khyla Schmidt, Khyla's Bookshelf

First Edition Publication Date: November 11, 2025

Printed in the United States of America

AUTHOR'S NOTE

Hello, Little Hillion,

Mistletoe & Naughty is a dark, Krampus romance. Everything you thought you knew about the Demon of Christmas, Santa, and Mrs. Claus has been turned on its head.

The North Pole is not a winter wonderland, but rather a dark and dreary hellscape. I did a lot of research on other winter monsters and demons to ensure that I did justice to the myths in this dark, cold world, but with my own unique twist.

Please Note: This is a dark, paranormal romance that is intended for mature audiences. This is not your warm and fuzzy holiday story; however, no children were actually harmed by Krampus.

Reader's discretion is advised.

xoxo,

KL Hill

Also by KL Hill

Masquerave

Coded in Control

Chained to Control

Knights of Cindervail

A Legion of Bane & Embers

Novelettes

Spinning Out of Control (A Masquerave Story)

Up From Below

For everyone inevitably stuck on the Naughty List—be naughtier.

CHAPTER 1

Nicolette

I, Nicolette Evergreen, have been called every name imaginable except for *nice*. I'm what you would consider a thief, a fraud, or, better yet, a con artist. This explains why I prefer to spend my time in my secluded cabin in the woods, scamming people out of money and having it sent directly to one of my many bank accounts, never to be heard from again.

I'm chasing the same thrill that an adrenaline junkie experiences when jumping out of airplanes, except mine is when I drag my victims deeper and deeper into my web of lies and deceit; the massive payouts keep me coming back for more.

The wind rages against the cabin, fiercely rattling the windows, as a blizzard approaches that will probably leave me stranded out here for weeks. Fortunately, I keep this place well stocked with all the essentials and more, and it's entirely powered by solar panels, thanks to my big payouts. I might be a criminal, but I still give a shit about the planet. Plus, it's entirely off the grid and the perfect place to hide out, whether I need to lay low or keep going in the pursuit of an endless cash flow.

Speaking of which, unfortunately, my latest scam has me lying even lower than usual for a few days, forcing me to go without some of my favorite snowed-in snacks since the family of the man I catfished hired a PI to trace me, and I don't want to risk getting caught and going to jail for fraud.

I'm too fucking pretty to prance around behind bars in an orange jumpsuit for years. Not to mention, it would clash with my red hair.

The roaring fire fills the room with its warm light and heat, a single stocking hangs from the hearth with my name embroidered on it, and my tiny FM radio plays the 24-hour Christmas station—my only attempts to add some Christmas cheer, which are failing miserably.

I don't mind spending the holidays alone, since I really don't have a choice after going no contact with my family years ago. I don't have a single real friend because of my profession, and the last serious relationship I had ended last Christmas Eve when my ex decided to drop down his ex's chimney and crawl right under her Christmas tree skirt.

And the icing on the fucking fruit cake? He had the audacity to ask me if I wanted to join them instead of exchanging gifts, like we originally planned, after he butt-dialed me—or cock-dialed, really—while she was screaming his name.

Talk about an insane game of white elephant.

I gracefully declined his offer before I drove over, slashed his tires, and busted out his headlights and windshield with a metal baseball bat. I was the embodiment of feminine rage, taking the directive for my revenge from that one country song, while contemplating his "goodbye" as in that other one. I've never intentionally killed anyone, but that night, I was willing to become the subject of a true crime documentary and chase another thrill.

Of course, like any man caught in the act, he tried to play the victim and threatened to press charges, but all it took was me threatening to call his ex's new 6'5" biker boyfriend and inform him of her extracurricular activities for him to second-guess his decision. And like the little bitch he is, he folded, and as far as I can tell from hacking into his shit, he's continued fucking her on the side for almost a year now.

That is, until I just sent screenshots and finally got the boyfriend involved. I have alerts set for any articles mentioning their names, and I expect to see one any day now.

Merry fucking Christmas to me.

Needless to say, the holiday season has been ruined for me more than once by a string of unfortunate events, and I honestly couldn't care less about it all now. And like any millennial would, I suppress my feelings and busy myself by hiding out here, stacking my bank account with money from assholes who think they can get away with cheating on their spouses.

Is it an honest living? Absolutely not. But, fuck, if it's not fun.

As a thirty-two-year-old woman who's been shit on more times than I can count, I deserve the right to fuck with men and their finances by convincing them to be my sugar daddy, all while waiting for it to blow up in their faces—especially when they try to cross a line with me. I DM their significant others with receipts, starting my plan of revenge and taking down every Chad and Brad who's begging for attention in my inbox. Like I said, it's fun to ruin other people's lives since mine has already been blown to bits again and again.

I curl up on the couch under my favorite quilt and dive into the latest dark romance I grabbed at the big box store—a little five-finger discount gift to myself—and let the crackle of the fire lull me to sleep.

Outside, the wind picks up, whistling around the house like a cyclone and blowing in every direction. They're calling for over a foot of snow tonight, not counting snow drifts. I plan to be stranded here for a few days, stretched out by the fire, finger-fucking myself to all the smut I'll read during this little winter staycation.

Hours have passed, and my eyelids grow heavy. The sound of the roaring wind drowns out all other noises, pulling me toward sleep. My head sinks into the down throw pillow as I roll onto my side, with the last thing I see before the world fades to black being the flames flickering back at me, licking the edge of the hearth.

I'm not in the darkness for very long before I start to dream. It's the same dream I've had for almost twelve years, and it always happens around this time of the year. I find myself walking down the hallway of the childhood home I left behind the moment I turned eighteen. With every step I take, it seems to stretch longer as I try to reach the window at the end.

Suddenly, I stumble forward, tripping on air, and my hands smack against the windowpane; the cold immediately seeps into my skin. The temperature around me plummets, frost creeping across the glass and blocking my view, with only the hauntingly dim moonlight filtering through. Pulling the sleeve of my sweater over my hand, I wipe away the thick layer of frost, where I'm met with more than just the night sky on the other side.

A shadowed face with eyes burning like hellfire stares back at me, baring its sharp teeth in a hungry, lupine smile. I should be terrified and run away, but I only lean in more, nearly pressing my nose against the glass. I hear the window unlock; a cold gust of wind swirls around me as it slides up beneath my palm. My heart pounds with anticipation as a clawed hand, adorned with golden rings, curls around the bottom, lifting it higher. Just as the creature on the other side is about to climb in and itself, I jolt away.

My eyes fly open, and my heart thunders in my chest, a deafening roar in my ears. An ice-cold breeze crawls across my skin, drying the sheen of sweat and leaving goosebumps in its wake. Pulling the blanket snug under my chin, I notice the fire has died down to embers, leaving only a faint glow and barely any heat.

I sit up, wrapping the blanket tighter around me as my teeth chatter so violently that my jaw starts to ache, then shuffle over to the stack of wood next to the hearth. Shadows fill the corners of the room, seeming to press down on me. The wind whistles as it rushes down the chimney, rogue snowflakes fluttering past and swirling around the room. The wind has blown a dusting of soot across the floor, where it begins to fade a few feet from the hearth.

My heart races in my chest, and I stand frozen as I examine the footprints lightly etched into the dust. It's as if someone—or something—came down the chimney and walked right out... except these are no ordinary footprints, but large hoofprints.

What the hell?

I press the heels of my palms to my eyes, trying to rid them of sleep, all the while convincing myself that this is just my mind playing tricks on me. Turning slowly, I look over my shoulder at the rest of the cabin, which is covered in a blanket of darkness—a void that can disguise any intruder who might have broken in.

The temperature in the room seems to drop even more the longer I stand here, my breath clouding in front of me. My eyes scan the room for the culprit, but none of the windows are open, and the door is closed and locked tight.

I must still be dreaming, and this is a new version of it, finally catching up to my adult life. Just like in the dream, I walk over to the front window and lift the cream curtain, only to find frost coating the inside of the glass, blocking my view. My hand trembles as I lift it to wipe the window clean with the corner of my blanket, spreading the condensation away, the glass glittering in the low firelight. Leaning forward, I look out the window, fully expecting to see the same glowing eyes. Instead, I'm met only with an endless night and the occasional snowflake landing on the glass as the snowstorm continues to roll in.

Letting out a ragged breath, I step back from the window, the curtain falling back into place. I scrub my hands over my face and return to the fireplace, carefully sliding new logs onto the embers and stoking the flames. The fire roars back to life, casting a warm glow into the room. I watch the flames as they lick at the hearth, the comforting heat warming my skin and pushing back the shadows that were inching closer.

But even as my body warms, I can't shake the chill that prickles at my nape, causing my hair to stand on end, as if I'm being watched. A shiver runs through me from the cold that feels like it's seeped deep into my bones. Sleep suddenly overtakes me and pulls me down onto the white faux fur rug laid out in front of the fire. The fur is soft beneath me, gently brushing my cheek as my wild red curls weave through it, resembling blood against the snow.

Curling my arm under my head, I listen to the crackle of the fire, like a sweet lullaby, lulling me back to sleep. But just as my eyes close and I begin to relax, I hear a faint click on the wood floor, like the heel of a shoe taking a tiny step into the room.

You're just hearing things, Nicolette.

That sound was nothing more than the fire crackling against the stone hearth or the wind trying to slip through the gaps under the door, pressing against it with all its might. My limbs grow heavy, and my eyes close, sending me tumbling back into my dreamscape to once again stare into the fiery eyes looking back at me from the other side of the window of my cabin. Its gaze consumes me, heating me from the inside out with a flame that threatens to burn me alive...and I just might let it.

CHAPTER 2

Nicolette

My body is stiff from the position I fell asleep in, and my shoulder and back throb as I sit up. The dull gray daylight filters through the curtains while the snowstorm rages outside, icy snowflakes pounding against the windowpanes.

Rubbing the sleep out of my eyes, I stretch my limbs and crack my back, trying to shake off the shitty night of sleep. My dreams of sugarplums quickly turned into nightmares of something banging on the door, with my hand just inches from the handle before it was blown off its hinges. Shadows swirled through the living room, blending with the violent storm outside as it rushed in, wrapping around me and forcing me to the floor. The shadows thickened, blocking me from the frigid wind, closing in and nearly stealing my breath. I woke up just as the shadows began to part, revealing whatever was hiding within them.

I kept drifting in and out of sleep throughout the night, aware that I was tending to the fire. Each time I fell back asleep, I found myself back beneath the shadows, their tendrils wrapping around me and holding me in place. I would feel their soft caress moving across my throat and down my sides, brushing gently beneath my breasts and down to my hips, causing heat to swirl in my lower abdomen and leaving me yearning for more every time I woke up.

I should have been fucking terrified, like any normal person would have been. But no, I was a horny bitch with her hand pressed between her legs, trying to find release in the short time my eyes were open. It was as if the nightmare didn't want it to go too far, as if it was controlling me—which sounds insane.

I've definitely been in isolation for too long already.

Regardless, it's been a while since I've been laid, and honestly, I'll take whatever I can get—dreaming or not.

I check the time on the mantle clock and see that it's only 6:30—much earlier than I'm used to waking up since my profession keeps me active late into the night. I wipe my hand across my face as I stand up and shuffle to the kitchen to brew a much-needed pot of coffee. As it drips, I scan the cabin, my eyes catching on soot that covers the floor around the fireplace, and I start to pale.

I swallow hard around the lump in my throat as I approach the scuff marks that break up the smooth layer of ash. This isn't caused by the wind blowing down the chimney when I let the fire get too low, and these are *not* human footprints—ruling out any suspicion of sleepwalking.

I lower myself and trace my finger through the soot around the unmistakable hoofprint that looks as though a huge horse trotted through here on near-silent feet.

What the fuck?

This must be a dream—it's got to be.

I pinch my arm hard and gasp in pain. Okay, I'm definitely not asleep. This feels very real and terrifying. Panic starts to overwhelm me, causing my knees to buckle as I suck in a shuddering breath.

Get your fucking shit together, Nicolette.

I step back and stare at the floor. There's a logical explanation for this... right? Maybe it's just the early signs of cabin fever. I've been alone for so long out here, and I'm starting to go stir crazy—that's all. Once I have some coffee and see a bit more daylight outside, I'll have a clearer mind about everything.

I grab the broom and dustpan from the closet, sweep up the soot, and dump it back into the fire, ridding myself of this insanity and ignoring the feeling of being watched that prickles up my spine.

Instead of spiraling, I take my time with my morning routine: drink my coffee, sear my skin in a quick hot shower, and then settle back on the couch to disassociate from the lingering thoughts and get lost in my book.

But no matter how hard I try, my mind won't focus on a single task. Instead, it's being pulled in a dozen different directions. I snap the book shut and drop it on the side table, trading it for my phone, where I pull up my bank account and double-check that all the zeros I've hustled for are still there.

The corners of my lips curl up at my most recent payout, the urge to pull off another heist almost driving me crazy—but it's still too soon. Even as I open the dating app, I know I need more time for things to settle, to make sure the trail leads to a dead end, not right to the front door of this cabin, and to remind myself not to get fucking greedy.

Well, *greedier.*

A cold gust of wind blows through the living room, and my head snaps up. My eyes flick to the still-roaring fire even as a shiver runs down my spine. Paranoia prickles across my skin, and I close out the app, ignoring the slew of unread messages, and toss the phone to the other side of the couch.

Nobody's coming for you; get the hell over yourself.

Dropping my head against the back of the couch, I run my hand over my face, squeezing my eyes shut as I press my thumb and finger against my eyelids until I see stars. I sit there in silence; the only sound filling the room is the roaring fire, and I let my thoughts drift. I lose track of time as I shuffle through memories of past Christmases, each one growing bleaker as the years pass, until the sound of a quiet thunk pulls me back to reality.

I raise my head slowly, my eyes fluttering back open, and expect it to be nothing more than my imagination or the wind rattling against the house. But the culprit of the sound is lying in the middle of my living room floor—a large, black rock. Except, it's not a rock—it's a fucking lump of coal.

I stare into the fireplace, my mind racing to find an explanation for why there's a lump of coal sitting in the middle of my living room, as if it's a ticking time bomb. My fireplace is wood-burning, and even if an ember had exploded, there would be a cloud of dust with pieces scattered across the floor. It wouldn't be so perfectly chiseled, as if it were recently plucked from the depths of the earth.

My eyes dart to the window, expecting it to be shattered, but I'm pretty sure I would have noticed if someone threw something through the glass. Not to mention, it would let in the storm that continues to rage outside.

It's no secret that I've fucked over a lot of people in my adult life, and maybe they've finally caught up to me. But every explanation I can come up with seems impossible—unless they dropped it down the chimney, and I would've definitely noticed someone stomping around on my roof. Plus, no one is stupid enough to climb up there in the middle of a blizzard. I'm in the middle of nowhere, on what would be a nearly impassable route in this weather, and completely off the grid. No one is finding me out here or online, with my various VPNs and satellite internet bouncing off the nearest ranger's tower, making me nearly untraceable.

I'm fucking smarter than that.

I reach down and pick up the piece of coal, feeling its weight in my palm. I bring it close to my face and examine it, though I'm not sure what I'm looking for. A message, maybe? Something to prove I'm not just making this up? I know the ghost stories and legends about these woods, and while I don't buy into the supernatural, I also realize there are things in this world we can't explain, and I'm not about to try and piss off some ancient entity.

I like it out here, and it would be a real bitch to have to pick up and move. I bought this cabin from a hunter's grandson, in cash, with no questions asked. It's the perfect size for someone like me, with an open living room and kitchen area, a small loft accessible by ladder, and a single bedroom with a full bath. I renovated it myself, keeping the outside looking as run-down as possible, while making the inside a cozy cottage in the woods—Sleeping Beauty style.

The wind picks up outside, and the wooden siding creaks from the impact as I slowly approach the front door and pull back the blackout curtain. I'm met with frosted glass and the dull morning light. I wipe my hand over the freezing glass, and the ice melts into liquid that drips down my fingers. The snow presses against the house, with drifts climbing up the surrounding trees, seeming to be waist deep.

Well, shit. I might be stuck here longer than I originally expected.

I narrow my gaze, searching for any tracks in the snow, but the fierce winds are the perfect accomplice for anyone trying to hide here. Taking a deep breath, I shake off the eerie feeling of being watched, just as my stomach growls loudly—maybe some food and more coffee will help take the edge off.

The bacon sizzles in the cast-iron skillet as I make another cup of coffee, loading it up with sweetener and creamer. I turn up the radio, letting the overly cheerful Christmas tunes drown out the sound of the howling wind, and focus my mind on something other than this creeping feeling at my back.

I tend to the cabin, making sure all drafty cracks are sealed and that I have everything I need for the next few days. Although it's a bit late to go into the outside cellar, a woman has to do what a woman has to do to survive, and if that means digging in the feet of snow for potatoes, then I will fight off the frostbite when that time comes.

The snow keeps piling up inch by inch throughout the day. The heavy clouds above prevent the sun from breaking through, making the already-short daylight hours feel as if it's been an endless night. Soon, all light disappears from outside, plunging the forest into darkness, with the space between the trees becoming depthless.

I close the curtains, taking a peek outside for any trespassers, and add more wood to the fire. The flames lick at the hearth, sending heat throughout the room. I settle back on the couch and curl up under a fleece throw, finally relaxing with my mind at ease for the first time today.

Another cold breeze slips through the space, sending a shiver down my spine. The hair on the back of my neck stands up as the wind grows louder, swirling around the cabin. The wooden supports creak as if they're buckling under the weight of the snow and ice. The radio crackles, cutting off the cheerful Christmas tune, and the static rises to a deafening volume before suddenly cutting out.

I rise to my feet, my body trembling in sync with my racing heart, while anxiety crawls across my skin like fire ants. The wind's roar suddenly ceases, as if someone hit a mute button on the storm. The wind, the crackling fire, and the cabin's creak all fall silent. I suck in a ragged breath, my legs refusing to move as

I remain frozen in place. My eyes flick to the front door and see that the deadbolt is still firmly locked.

I take another steadying breath, the air fogging in front of me as the temperature plummets. Just as I manage to calm my racing heart, the door begins to shudder as if someone is pounding on it from the other side, and the sound floods the room at full volume. I cover my ears and cringe, my red curls falling over my face as I duck my head down until everything settles again, and the room is filled with the haunting melody of "I'll Be Home for Christmas" from the radio.

I slowly look back up at the door and gasp as I see the glow of a red eye peering through the small crack in the curtains hanging over the front door's window.

Watching me.

Suddenly, the front door swings open as a blood-curdling scream escapes my lips, echoing through the room as I fall backward onto the couch. The cold wind and snow blow in around a large figure as its hooved foot clacks on the wood floor; the hardwood creaks under its weight, threatening to buckle.

"Nicolette Evergreen," a deep voice echoes through the swirling storm, my name ringing out in the cabin. The wind shifts and the snow clears, revealing a monster beneath the blanket of white.

It stands nearly eight feet tall, with thick black horns curling out of its head, surrounded by long black hair that falls past its shoulders. Gold piercings decorate its pointed ears, sparkling in the light. Its lips, pulled into a malicious-looking smile, are adorned with snake bite piercings—gold loops pulling tight against its skin.

The upper half of its massive body is covered in an array of tattoos, symbols, and characters I don't recognize, with a black leather harness crisscrossing over its torso, seemingly the only thing keeping in the packed muscles beneath its dark gray skin.

Its chest is broad, its nipples pierced, and long, muscular arms end in black, clawed fingertips adorned with gold rings. Tight, black leather pants slim down its legs, revealing black fur that ends in enormous hooves as it steps further into the cabin.

Its eyes are black, except for its irises, which burn bright red like hellfire, and they seem strangely familiar to some I've seen before.

"W-who the fuck are you?" I try to spit out the words, but they're breathless, as if the air has been sucked from the room, fear clawing up my throat.

The monster's lips curl into a devilish grin as it kicks the front door shut, its sharp teeth glowing red from the fire's flames, chuckling darkly. "Your *nightmare* before Christmas."

CHAPTER 3

Nicolette

My body trembles as the monster watches me, its face still twisted into a malicious grin, its eyes gleaming in the firelight. "You've been a very, *very* naughty girl, Nicolette," it says in its low, smooth voice, the flames of the fire flickering with every word. "And I'm here to cash in on the debt of your deeds."

My hands scrape against the wood floor as I scramble back into the kitchen. "Tell me who the fuck you are," I screech as I reach up and grip the counter, pulling myself to my feet without taking my eyes off the monster. I yank a large knife from the butcher block, quickly raise it over my head, and fling it across the room.

All my practice with chopping wood and teaching myself the art of axe throwing over the years gives me confidence that whatever the fuck this thing is, it will be dead in just a few seconds from my blade lodging itself right between its eyes.

The knife flies through the air, seeming to land right on target, but at the last second, the monster reaches out, and its long, black-tipped fingers curl around the handle, stopping it just inches from its face.

My heart drops into my stomach as its devilish grin widens, revealing sharp teeth while it chuckles darkly. Its long, forked tongue flicks from its lips, grazing the blade, as if slicing it open on purpose. Blood coats the edge of the blade and drips from the tip of its tongue. Its sharp teeth are stained with crimson as it casually tosses the knife into the air, catching it once again by the handle.

"You are a *very* naughty girl for that, Nicolette." Its eyes flash. "And do you know what happens to naughty girls like you this time of year?"

I keep my eyes on the monster as I pull another knife from the block, my fingers curling tightly around the handle of the serrated blade, prepared to throw it if it makes another move. My heart pounds loudly in my chest, rattling my bones as the creature takes a deep breath through its nose—seemingly inhaling my scent. Its smile widens as it says, "They're chained, whipped, and *punished.*"

Holding the knife between us, with the sharp tip ready to impale, I stand my ground. "Get the fuck out of my cabin or I'll fucking *kill* you."

That same cold breeze I've been feeling seems to crawl up my body and wrap around my neck, like a phantom hand. The cold fingers press into my throat, choking the air from my lungs. I drop the knife, where it lands with a clatter, as I desperately try to grasp the invisible hand, but I only manage to scratch my own throat. I blink, trying to clear the darkness that edges into my vision while the monster moves toward me. Its eyes burn and flicker in the firelight.

It grips my hair, claws scraping across my scalp as it yanks my head back to look up at it, the phantom hand loosening its grip slightly. I suck in a breath, ready for it to tighten again, but it just holds me like that, pressing its invisible fingers into my throat. My breathing becomes erratic as I stare up at the monster licking its lips, prepared to eat me alive.

"Who are you?" I choke out from around the phantom palm pressing against my throat. "And what the fuck do you want from me?"

The monster chuckles, the sound echoing as if it's inside my mind, slamming the knife tip into the countertop. "All I want for Christmas is *you*, Nicolette. *All of you*."

My eyes widen as its free hand brushes my cheek, the golden rings on its fingers icy to the touch. "Leave me alone," I sob, the realization that I'm alone in the middle of the woods and a monster has me in its grip settling into my chest, choking me as much as the phantom hand that still holds me firmly by the throat. "If you're here to rob me, take whatever you want. Just please... leave."

The monster steps closer, its breath warm against my skin as it whispers, "You act as though I am nothing more than a stranger to you, Nicolette, when I have visited you every chance I could get. I always knew when you were sleeping and when you were awake." He pulls back. The endless depths of his eyes draw me in, and I find myself getting lost in the blackness.

My eyes flutter closed, and the next thing I know, I'm standing at the end of the long hallway—the same one that's been in my dreams for nearly half my life, but this time, it's not a window at the end, but the monster.

"Tell me who you are right the fuck now." My voice echoes down the hall, bouncing all around me.

The monster tilts its head to the side, watching me with curiosity. "You really don't recognize me?" it asks as it steps toward me, and in a flash, it's on me again. "After all these years?" It tsks, the same monstrous grin spreading across its face, showing its sharp teeth. "Then I suppose I need to remind you."

The image of the hallway fades away, and I find myself back in my cabin, standing in my kitchen. Its long tongue gently glides across my jaw, sending a shiver down my spine as a familiar warmth ignites inside me. I gasp at the sensation, and a flush creeps up my neck.

Its free hand grips my waist, claws pricking my skin as it pulls me closer. "I'm the dark companion to the jolly Saint you all worship and hold in such high regard, but where he allegedly gives, I get to *take*," it whispers, its words filling my mind with images of whips and chains as the sounds of moans fill my ears.

My moans.

"You're... *Krampus*?" I choke on the words. This is unbelievable. I must still be dreaming and have clearly read too many monster romance books if this is the kind of shit I'm into.

It grins, curling its fingers tighter through my hair as I glance at its sharp cheekbones and chiseled jaw. "While that is the name mortals have given me throughout the centuries, you, little vixen, can call me Kryx. But only *you*."

My mouth falls open. "You... you've been the one in my dreams all this time, haven't you? The one watching me through the window." But how? How is this even possible? They were just dreams.

Weren't they?

He bares his teeth, running his tongue along the sharp edges. "That other fucker isn't the only one watching the people on his list." His claws press against my skin, pricking me and sending a shiver down my spine. "And you are at the *top* of mine."

I swallow hard to suppress the lump in my throat. "But... why are you here?" My eyes scan the countertop, looking for a weapon or anything I can use to defend myself. Those crimson eyes belong to a predator, and I'm his fucking prey.

His laugh is as dark as the storm ridden sky. "Because it's finally time to cash in for all the naughty things you've done in your life, and for every debt, I intend to leave a mark."

He presses his center against mine, his length hardening between us, pushing into my stomach. "Please," I whisper, the only word I seem able to choke out. And I don't know if it's begging as my body betrays me, or a plea as fear crawls beneath my skin.

He drags his sharp teeth across my skin, running his tongue along the sensitive area of my neck. "*More*, Nicolette. I've always loved it when you *begged* for me, especially in your dreams, and I love it even more now that you're here in front of me, saying it out loud."

His large body cages me against the kitchen counter. I look into his fiery gaze, and as if his words were a sledgehammer breaking a dam, my mind floods with images that could only come from dark, repressed dreams. Images of this exact monster holding me down and doing every other deed but actually fucking me.

His long, forked tongue flicks over every inch of my body, pushing me over the edge again and again, not bothering to catch me as I fall but grabbing my hair and yanking me back to him. Heat floods my core, making my clit pulse as if it has been zapped by electricity. My body seems to hum, my muscles ache, and my skin prickles—craving to be touched... by him.

I blink, and the images fade, pulling me back to the cabin, still caught between him and the counter. I press my hands against his hard, muscular chest, trying to push him away, but he doesn't move. I try to deny that he's been haunting my dreams, but now that my mind feels clear, I can recall many times I've woken up with my fingers between my legs, an orgasm washing over me.

All because of *him*.

The Christmas demon, who is akin to the devil, has been appearing in my dreams and watching me for almost my entire adult life. *Waiting.* He's as familiar as the monsters lurking in my closet, along with the ones slithering under my bed, threatening to grab me by the ankles and pull me under to eat me alive.

My mind screams at how fucked up this is, but my body has other ideas—recreating the devious things he's already done to me, which seem to be hidden deep in my mind, far out of reach and buried beneath the trauma that already consumes my thoughts.

"You're a sick fuck," I snap, clawing at his skin, desperately trying to push him away and attempting to reach for the knife that's just out of reach. "Stalking me and trying to take over my mind. How *dare* you do that to me?"

He lowers his head, pressing his nose against mine, forcing me to look at him as the phantom hand around my throat tightens, while others seem to grip my arms and legs, holding me in place. "That's not what you were saying when you willingly let me into your dreams, and that's certainly not what you're thinking now," he growls, the rumble vibrating through me. Heat begins to curl in my lower abdomen. "Lying will only make your punishment that much worse, Nicolette, and it's already going to have you *begging*."

CHAPTER 4

Nicolette

Kryx pulls away from me before swiftly slinging me over his shoulder like Santa's sack of toys. I pound my fists against his back, yelling at him to put me down as he roughly grips my ass and heads to the bedroom, barely squeezing both of us through the door frame.

Dropping me onto the bed, I bounce on the mattress and use the force to try to scramble back up. As I reach the edge of the mattress, something cold grips my wrist and yanks me back, pulling me flat on my back. The same cold bite encircles my other wrist, securing both my arms above my head and tying them to the headboard. I look up and see chains wrapped around each wrist, rattling with every failed attempt to free myself.

"Let. Me. Go." I force out the words with each yank, thrusting my hips for leverage. But I'm just left gasping, a bead of sweat sliding down my temple as panic seeps in with every heaved breath, paralyzing my body.

He acts as if I should know him—as if all those times I saw him and let him in, I wanted him. But that can't be possible. He's a monster—a *demon*—and he's no more real than Santa Claus.

He's nothing more than a story told to children to keep them being good, for goodness' sake. And even as my body betrays me and seems drawn to him like a moth to a flame, I can't just let him do this.

This has to be another dream—a nightmare—with my stir-crazy mind playing tricks on me.

Kryx stands at the end of the bed, surrounded by darkness, except for the fiery glow from the flames in the living room, flickering around the hearth like a caged animal begging to be set free, singeing the toe of my single stocking that still hangs from it. He snaps his fingers, and the candles on my dresser light up, casting a soft glow in the room and creating shadows on the sharp lines of his face, making him seem more devious than before.

He places a knee on the mattress, the wooden bed creaking under his weight. His burning eyes wander over my body, examining every inch as if he's done it a thousand times. He slowly slides a finger up the inside of my leg, across my center, and hooks it onto the waistband of my jogger sweatpants.

"*Wait,*" I yip, just as he yanks them down, ripping them from my body and discarding them like nothing more than old rags. The smell of ash fills my nostrils as his claws glide over my skin and begin to trace the edge of my panties.

"Are you wet for me, Nicolette?" he croons, lowering his head between my legs and inhaling deeply. "Your needy cunt has always begged for me."

His long tongue glides over the thin material, the only thing between his mouth and my aching pussy, tasting me. He groans as I whimper, his claw tearing through the fabric and shredding it into ribbons, while, once again, the smell of ash fills the air. His warm breath gently brushes my center as his massive hands push against the inside of my thighs, spreading my legs wide.

"*Please,*" I moan. It should be a demand, my body betraying me again, but the word cracks as it slips from my lips.

How fucked up this is?

I've supposedly been getting off to this monster, who has been stalking my dreams for years, and who has apparently been using some magic to hide it from me. I should be terrified, but none of the depictions of Krampus have been accurate, because this monster from Hell shouldn't be this... *hot*. It's as if he's taken my extremely toxic type and injected it with hellfire.

His lifetime of experience shows as he runs his tongue over my folds, circling my entrance before thrusting his forked tongue into me. The chains tighten around my wrists, holding me in place even more as my back arches and my toes curl while I gasp for breath.

He drags his tongue out, flicking it across my aching clit, and growls into my center as I try to press my legs together. I freeze as he keeps slowly licking and sucking my pussy, as if he needs to taste every inch of it. He seems to know exactly what will drive me wild, as if this isn't the first time he's been between my legs. And if what he showed me is true, then he should know it as well as the back of his hand.

He pulls back just enough to lift his head, his horns gleaming in the firelight as his eyes heat up, scanning my body. "For someone rotten to the core, you taste so fucking sweet." He licks his lips, coated with my desire, making his lip piercings shine even more, before dropping his head back down to continue devouring me.

"Fuck," I hiss as he lashes my clit with his tongue like a whip, his sharp teeth scraping against my sensitive skin. The feeling is almost unbearable as it floods through me. Heat races through my veins as I teeter on the edge of pain and pleasure— my body prepared to surrender to oblivion. My breaths become ragged, my back arches just as I'm about to come, then... *nothing*.

I cry out in frustration, my body burning with the need for release as that fucking monster looks up at me with a devilish grin. "What the *fuck?*" I scream, my legs trembling in his hold, the prick of his nails forcing me to stay still.

He chuckles darkly, the sound curling around and dragging its fingers through my thick, red curls. "I told you that I was here to dole out your punishment. Did you really think you'd get to climb the mountain of pleasure without the pain?"

He really is a fucking monster. *"Fuck you,"* I bite.

"Soon, but not yet," he purrs. "I like to play with my food, and you, my little vixen, are a fucking treat."

His claws glide over my inner thigh, the sharp prick of pain cutting through me as it heightens the pleasure he had denied me. His sharp teeth flash just before sinking into my skin, a scream ripping from my throat just as I fall over the edge, coming harder than I ever have before. His long tongue swirls over the mark, licking the blood from my skin.

His groan vibrates through me. "So fucking delicious."

The chains rattle as they slowly snake away, vanishing into thin air, leaving my arms hanging limply above my head. Kryx rises from between my legs, licking my cum from his lips— wasting not a single drop. He climbs over me, placing his large hands on either side of my head as his dark, soulless eyes stare down at me.

"I have waited far too long to taste you in this realm, little vixen." His voice is rough, his warm breath dancing across my skin. "And it's been worth every fucking minute."

His face hovers over mine, and his tongue darts out, flicking against my lips. The taste of my cum slips into my mouth. "Why are you doing this?" I ask in a rough whisper. "Why me?"

He grins like a schoolboy ready to share his deepest, darkest secret. "I was sent to punish someone else in your home, but that's when you caught me lurking on the rooftop. I knew you believed it to be a dream because no one in their right mind would have stayed silent and turned away. I am, after all, a living nightmare."

The shadows in the corners of the room shift and bend as if coming alive at the sound of his voice—the same voice that sends a chill up my spine. My mouth hangs open as he shifts his weight, his hand palming my breast, his thumb swiping over my sensitive nipples, sending pleasure straight to my core.

"So, you've been watching me since then?" I grit out, trying to ignore his touch as it ignites my skin, making me squirm beneath him. "And who were you there for? If what you're saying is true, only adults would have been there, and you're supposed to only go after children."

He pinches my nipple, causing me to gasp as he runs his tongue up my jaw and scrapes his teeth below my ear. A flush spreads across my face, burning my cheeks. "Do you believe everything you're told, little vixen? I pegged you as a smarter human than that. Of course, I've been *dreaming* of the day you peg me, but until then, this will have to do."

I squirm, trying to wiggle free as he slides his knee between my legs, his leather pants roughly brushing against my exposed pussy. "Why are you really here?" I pant as phantom hands grip my wrists, once again pinning them above my head. "What do you want from me?"

"I've been skipping over you for quite some time, and it was about time to collect, or else the big man in red might finally notice, and it's better if you're not on his radar." He drags his nose down the column of my neck. "You never did anything *too* naughty to justify moving you up the list, until this week, when you drained that man's entire savings account, his retirement, and stole his assets, all while blackmailing him and sending screenshots of his infidelity to his wife, ultimately ruining his life."

My whole body stiffens as he lays everything out in front of me. "Fuck you and fuck him," I spit. "He was looking for it and approached me. I'm not one to pass up a business opportunity. It's not my fault he's a cheating asshole, and I can't help it if he got in too deep. His wife was catching on anyway, so I just helped a girl out."

He stares down at me, his eyes blazing as he quirks a brow. "Don't act so innocent, little vixen. Your vigilantism didn't quite hit its mark, now did it? The more you do things like that, the longer I get to stay—get to explore." He gives me a wink before his hand glides down my sweatshirt to the hem, sliding it underneath. "It's his fucking fault. He threatened to report me to the police," I say, trying to steady my trembling voice. "I had no choice but to out his sorry ass and go into hiding."

He pushes my sweatshirt up, exposing my breasts, and the cool room air tightens my sensitive buds. "And yet, you didn't bat an eye about any of it, did you? Your bank account was full, and you moved on to your next victim. Tell me, who's the naughty one again?"

His teeth scrape across my breast, causing me to arch my back and push my nipple into his waiting mouth. His tongue circles it, flicking across my skin like a whip, prompting a moan that makes me shove my head back into the mattress.

"What about *him*?" I ask, nearly breathless as he continues his assault on my breasts, his clawed fingers trailing across my ribs.

"Who?"

"That fucker who tried to rat me out. Surely adultery is enough to put him on your list," I say, nearly breathless. "Did you suck his dick like you ate my pussy? Leave him with blue balls out in the cold?"

He gives me a malicious grin, his eyes flaring like embers. "Oh, don't you worry, little vixen. He got more than a lump of coal for his actions. And I can promise that he didn't enjoy his punishment nearly as much as you're going to enjoy yours."

CHAPTER 5

Nicolette

I squeeze my eyes shut as a vivid image flashes in my mind of the man I catfished, chained and face down on a bench as Kryx tortures him, leaving angry, red lash marks across his skin. My heart races as his screams of agony echo, pulsing against the inside of my skull, and a sheen of sweat covers my skin as I watch this man be punished for a deed I had a hand in. I should be terrified, and yet, I'm turned on.

So fucking turned on.

My pussy pulses as he keeps dragging his claws down my sides, and goosebumps cover my skin. This demon has been haunting my dreams for years, exploiting me while I sleep. I should be utterly disgusted, but I can't stop trying to recall more memories of the filthy, naughty things I let him do to me, which make me blush and heat me to the core. I guess in some fucked-up way, I did consent to him being there, and I have the faintest idea that I only encouraged his malicious acts.

Yeah, that sounds about right.

The bindings around my wrists loosen, and I reach up to touch one of his horns, sliding my finger down the ribbed, black bones. He groans, the sound so deep it vibrates through the bed —and through me.

I wrap my fingers around the curve, and he lets out a hiss, his body tensing as I glide my hand up and down, treating it like it were his hard cock in one of my lucid dreams. There, he's rough but careful. He finds the perfect balance of pain and pleasure that keeps me begging for more, but even as the memories come back, shattered like glass I'm trying to piece together, there's a part of me that feels empty and still longs for more.

"Little vixen," he moans. "You're playing a *dangerous* game."

Reality creeps back in, the flashes of my dreams fading as I reach for them. Instead, a sense of impending doom fills the empty space in my chest, making my heart race. I need to get him off me and run. He's like a worm on a hook, trying to lure me in—drag me into whatever fucked-up relationship that already seems to exist.

If I were to escape, where would I even go?

The ranger's station? Like they would do anything.

A hotel? That sounds a bit more realistic, if I don't freeze to death in the several feet of snow covering the forest—the same snow my car is stuck under. Still, it's miles and miles to the nearest ranger station or another cabin, and there wouldn't be enough time to grab my emergency bag or dig myself out.

But my fucked-up family didn't raise a pussy, now did they?

A grin pulls at my lips as his pupils flare, his body tensing more as I reach up with my free hand and grip his other horn, running both up and down in unison. If I can get him off like this, maybe he'll fall asleep, and I can make my escape. I put on my video face, licking and biting my bottom lip.

"So, jolly ole Saint Nick gets the fun job, and you have to do all this physical labor, huh?" I say in a low, teasing tone as I continue stroking him.

His widened eyes snap up, meeting mine. His body becomes even more rigid as he slides his hand up the neck of my shirt and covers my mouth, pressing his large palm against my lips. "Do not speak his name aloud, *ever*. He sees you when you're sleeping, and he knows when you're awake, but if you speak of him as a believer, you feed into his power. While he's portrayed as a nice and jolly man, he's *far* from it." His eyes flash, viciously swirling like the storm outside. "The North Pole is a dark place, little vixen, full of monsters and evil spirits, and he's *no* different."

My eyes widen as he slides his hand away from my lips, wrapping it around my throat while my mouth gapes. "But wasn't he a real man who loved children and left them toys? Or is that a lie, too?"

He tilts his head to the side, his free hand continuing to explore my body, pressing his fingers into my curves and full hips. "He was a man once, yes. But that was centuries ago. As he aged, he sought immortality, abandoning every moral he ever held, and made a deal that left a dark mark on his soul. He is vastly different from the rosy-cheeked, plump man mortals have come to love and admire."

His eyes flick toward the door as if he's waiting for someone to burst through it, then he pulls his gaze back to me. "He didn't come to rule the North Pole with kindness and goodwill toward men, but with the ruthlessness of a mad king who will stop at nothing to be the most powerful being between Hell and Earth. He and his missus trap and use those they see as threats or are desperately alone, treating them as nothing more than toys."

I stare back at him as shadows close in around us, darkening the room. What the actual fuck? Santa Claus, the jolly man who brings gifts to children's houses, rides in a sleigh, and has adorable elves make the toys, is evil? What's next? The Easter Bunny is a man-eating monster who steals children?

"And if you think the elves he has enslaved are like those depicted in your stories, you'd be very, very wrong," he says lowly, as if he read my mind. Can he? If he can slip so easily into my dreams and do who knows what, then surely, he can read my mind, right?

My brows furrow as I watch him, his eyes fixed on where his hand rests on my throat. "Can you read my mind?"

He laughs, the sound circling me like a shark in bloody water. "No, little vixen. However clever you believe yourself to be, you reveal your curiosity on your face. You are an open book."

My brows knit together, and my nose scrunches. I am clever, you motherfucker. How else would I be so successful in conning people out of their money if I weren't? But I don't need to explain myself to him, this monster, because once he's done with... whatever this is, I'll be going right back to raking in the cash and living my best life. Maybe next time, I'll disappear to an island and hide away in a secluded beach town, living on rum and the freshest seafood.

"How did you get into my dreams?" I ask, my voice strained from the lump in my throat.

His eyes seem to swirl, their inky black depths like a dark sea ready to drag me under. "I simply knocked, and you let me in," he says casually, as if that's completely normal.

He shifts, and I hear the clink of chains just as the cold bite of metal grips my wrists again, pulling them away from his horns and back up over my head. He runs his tongue over his sharp teeth as his eyes darken. "Don't think I didn't notice that you left the front door unlocked tonight. As if knowing that even a blizzard wouldn't stop me, and it only made it that much easier for me to get to you."

I blink in disbelief. I *never* leave the door unlocked. I'm way too paranoid for that, even in a remote forest. There's no fucking way...

I gasp as he presses his hardening length against my center, his leather pants the only barrier between us. Something cold, like a winter wind, begins to tighten around my thighs and pulls my knees up, keeping my legs spread open and my pussy exposed.

I look down and see that his shadows have been binding me, tightening with each move I make as if they're a boa constrictor. "You have always begged for me, Nicolette, and I want not only to hear you beg... but I want to hear you scream."

He slides off me and steps to the end of the bed, his massive body looming over me. I try to steady my breathing, but the anticipation rushes through my veins as a leather flogger appears in his hand, his fingers gripping the handle tightly. I struggle against the shadow bindings, but it's useless. "No, please," I gasp. "What are you doing? *Wait.*"

Running the tendrils through his palm, he gives me a wicked smile just as he whips them against my thigh, right over the bite mark he left. I cry out in pain, but my body keeps betraying me as my pussy pulses with need just as he snaps it against my other thigh. I let out another cry as he moves back and forth, heat pooling between my legs—*dripping.*

He runs his fingers up my center, coating them with my desire, before he brings them to his lips—his long, forked tongue licking them clean. "Fucking *delicious,*" he groans, bringing them back to tease my entrance. "I could eat you for every fucking meal."

I squirm, and he makes me pant like a bitch as he pulls his fingers away, sliding the tendrils of the flogger through my folds. With a flick of his wrist, he flogs my pussy, and my back arches off the bed as I let out another cry. Pain mixes with pleasure as he pushes me toward the edge with every strike until he finally stops.

My breath is heavy, and my thighs burn with both pain and desire, causing my inner walls to clench. I feel the warm leather handle at my entrance, and I whimper as he pushes it in inch by inch before slowly pumping it in and out of me.

"Please, fuck me," I beg, barely recognizing my pleas as the last specks of my self-respect fade away. "I'll be a good girl, I promise."

He chuckles darkly and keeps teasing me with the handle. "Naughty girls don't get to make demands, especially lying ones."

He uses his free hand to tug at the laces of his leather pants, his cock springing free, and I can't stop the groan that escapes me at the sight of his hard length in front of me. It's long and thick, with a dark onyx tip—the color of his hooves—that fades down his shaft to the charcoal gray of his skin. Silver balls glint along the underside, like bells, from the Jacob's Ladder piercings that climb up him. Precum drips from the tip like melting snow as he pumps his hand up and down the length, the thick vein underneath pulsing.

Holy shit. My mouth waters as I imagine what he might taste like, and I start to pant as the pleasure between my legs intensifies with every thrust of the handle, matching his rough strokes up and down his length.

He pulls the handle out, flips it in his hands, and slaps the flogger against my clit. The sudden pain causes my eyes to roll back and my body to convulse as I come instantly. I scream as he does it again, each time a little softer as I ride the wave of my orgasm. I draw in a ragged breath, my body trembling as he keeps me tightly bound in his chains and shadows.

The mattress dips as he leans onto it. I can hear his soft grunts and look down to see his cock glistening, the veins bulging as his strokes become erratic. His head falls back slightly before he lets out a growl, his cum shooting across my abdomen, sliding down my skin, and cascading over my pussy.

His dark eyes seem to lighten as he looks down at me, licking his lips and huffing in a deep breath, causing his large chest to expand. "Such a dirty girl, covered in a demon's hot cum." He growls, running his fingers over my skin, smearing himself up to my chest and all over his fingers. "A fucking mess."

He leans further forward, smearing his cum-coated fingers across my lips. And as if on instinct, I open my mouth and stick out my tongue, licking them clean. I groan at the taste of him and begin to salivate at the thought of swallowing every last drop.

What has fucking come over me? Is this one of my fucked-up dreams?

My body is begging for him, and my mind strains as if I should recall something about him that has been lost in the darkest corners of my mind—an echo so faint, as if the wind is carrying it away.

"You like that, don't you, little vixen?" He smirks. "I'll have to remember that for next time."

Next time?

The shadows suddenly vanish, followed by the chains, leaving my legs and arms to go limp. My body is nothing but gelatin, making it impossible to run, even if I wanted to.

He slips off the bed and steps back, admiring his handiwork. He smirks and rounds the corner, lifting me and carrying me to my small bathroom. His corded, muscular arms hold me high above the floor. He gracefully ducks through the doorway, his horns nearly grazing the doorframe, and carefully sets me down.

"Clean yourself up, little vixen. But hurry, I don't have all night," he says, his heated gaze looking me over from head to toe before the door clicks shut behind me.

I turn to look at myself in the mirror, and my cheeks heat at the person staring back. I'm covered in cum—his smeared across my chest and stomach, and mine dripping down my thighs. My fiery-red hair is tousled in all directions, and my face and chest are flushed, giving my cheeks a rosy glow. The curls around my face are tight and damp, a sheen of sweat glistening across my forehead. I step away from the vanity and look down, the bite mark on my leg bright red, with all the blood licked clean from it, making it look like it's already healing.

I think about how it will scar and shake the insane thought of wanting it to leave a permanent mark. It's fucking insane to want to have a mark left by a demon, *especially* by Krampus... er, *Kryx*.

While yes, he bears similarities to the horrifying depictions of the monster that allegedly steals naughty children and whips them, he is nothing like the stories we've been told. Has he been stalking me for most of my adult life, and has he broken into my dreams? Yes, but he isn't looking at me as if he wants to kill me or drag me to Hell; instead, he seems to want to destroy me in a very different way. Even his depthless eyes don't look at me like a monster's would, but as if he's been starving through a long, cold winter.

I turn on the shower, letting the hot water pour over my body and wash away any traces of him. I can't help but think what would happen if I let it soak into my skin, seep into my bones, and fuse to my soul. Would it poison and kill me or bring my tattered heart back to life?

I quickly scrub myself with my loofah, not wasting any time, my pale skin reddening, watching as the suds slide down and circle the drain. After a few minutes, I step out of the bathroom in my robe, and I am met with his hard, muscular body leaning against the doorframe. He gives me a once-over, his eyes flashing. Without a word, he scoops me into his arms again, this time holding me close as we head back to my bedroom.

The cabin is warm, with a fire that has clearly been rebuilt, along with the wood burner in my bedroom. He gently lays me onto the bed as if I'm a swaddled baby he's trying not to wake. His touch is tender as he pulls the covers over me, brushing my hair away from my face. He snaps his fingers, and all the lights go out, leaving only a soft glow from the fires.

"You can stay if you want," I say, my voice low. "I promise

not to bite... unless you want me to." I give him a wink, letting my lips pull up into a smirk.

He stands as still as a statue, his muscles hard as stone as he looms over me. "Sleep, little vixen. You're going to need all the rest you can get."

I open my mouth to object, but he lifts his hand, unfurls his fingers, and blows a long breath across his palm. What looks like glittery snow floats through the air, prickling against my face as it lands on my cheeks. Almost instantly, my eyes grow heavy, and the room starts to darken.

My body relaxes into the mattress, and the pleas for him to stay fade on my tongue as sleep overtakes me, pulling me into darkness. The same darkness that swirls through his eyes, snuffing out the hellfire that burns within them, leaving me to sleep in heavenly peace.

CHAPTER 6

Kryx

T he return to the North Pole is fucking exhausting. After crossing the barrier—which still feels like being stabbed by a thousand needles even after centuries— I'm faced with those relentless little elves who think that just because they work for Nick, they're above me on the food chain. No matter how many of them I tear apart with my bare hands, they seem to multiply faster than the Easter Bunny when it's in heat.

My hooves sink into the snow as I approach the looming, snow-capped castle sitting high in the middle of this desolate hellscape. The reindeer are scattered across the courtyard, their red eyes burning with the same hellfire that brought them to life. It's almost laughable how humans can see these vile creatures as gentle companions. While the mortal kind that herd far south are something to be fond of, these monsters will do more than bite the hand that feeds them.

However, those same humans believe Nick is still a jolly saint, but that part of him melted away when he sold his soul.

Thanks to that deal, I became involved in the trade and had to assist him while keeping a close eye as he grew stronger.

Now, we are seen as two sides of the same coin. Usually, I'm left to my own devices and follow the list. Still, tonight, the magic that binds us was working overtime to pull me back to this fucking wasteland, disrupting the time I had set aside for Nicolette.

Whatever the prick needs, it clearly couldn't wait.

My hooves click against the snow-covered stone steps, and the doors swing open magically as I approach. The warmth inside pulls me in so strongly that I nearly stumble over my own feet, but I manage to steady myself against the doorframe before falling flat on my face.

I walk down the long hallway, the large sconces on the wall flickering with each step, as if signaling me to move forward. They are decorated with holly wreaths and mistletoe, and between each one is a tapestry illustrating Nick's life story leading up to his trade for immortality. They're vivid with shades of red, blue, and green.

This main hallway differs from the rest of the fortress, which is decorated with tapestries showing the man as he is now, the self-proclaimed king of the North Pole. His cruelty knows no limits, and even though I am one of his counterparts—viewed as the winter devil—he has become so powerful that he makes the decisions and has more blood on his hands than any mere mortal could fathom.

I used to admire his ruthlessness and take part in his so-called "reindeer games," but lately, I can't even match the blood-lust that seems to have taken over him. His wife, Clara, is just as nefarious, using the elves to do her bidding and bring her unsuspecting humans to have her way with, all while Nick watches, getting drunk on winterberry wine. Those humans are either now enslaved to her or dead, buried under the snow, never to be seen again.

While I enjoy using my whips and chains on human pieces of shit, even I have to admit that their methods are quite unorthodox. Whatever they were in their human lives has long since burned up like coal in a fire.

Rounding the corner, I hear the tinkling of bells in the Great Hall, the last bit of truth connected to the saint that Nick used to be. I step through the threshold, and the doors swing wide, the frozen elves used as doorstops holding them in place.

I look around and see Nick sitting at the end of his long banquet table, wearing a crimson tunic and a leather harness strapped across his chest with his sleeves pushed up, revealing his corded forearms. He doesn't resemble the image humans have come to know of Santa Claus; instead, he's packed tightly with muscle, with his long white hair half pulled up into a loose bun at the back of his head and a short, trimmed white beard.

Clara, his wife, sits to his right as they enjoy their nightly feast, with her newest human pet on his knees beside her. He stares straight ahead, his eyes glazed over as he's lost in the trance she's put him in, while she gently pets his long brown hair. He's only wearing a pair of black leather briefs and a black collar with a leash clipped to the O-ring, the end of it looped around her wrist, as if he could actually run from her.

Clara is a beautiful woman, with her thick, reddish-brown hair styled in a coronet braid, reminiscent of a crown. Her skin is pale, dotted with freckles across the bridge of her nose. Her eyes are a deep green, like evergreen needles, and just as sharp. She's tall, with long, graceful limbs visible under her long red velvet robe.

However, her beauty only runs skin deep, and she's far more dangerous than most would give her credit for.

She catches my gaze and offers a knowing smile before snapping her long, delicate fingers. Her human pet crawls on his hands and knees beneath the table. She spreads her legs and leans back in her chair, her hands gripping the armrests as her eyes flutter shut. Nick barely seems to notice or doesn't care, as he'll probably join in whenever he's ready or just keep enjoying the show.

Nick's eyes flicker up to mine, and he gives me a vicious grin that mirrors that of a wolf at the edge of the forest, blood dripping from its maw. He stands suddenly, and the sound of his chair scraping across the stone echoes throughout the room. "Come, Kryx. Tonight, we drink!" His voice carries through the rafters, bouncing across the large room.

I mirror his smile, playing into his game as I approach the table. The elves rush to pull out my chair, the place setting already prepared for me. "What's the occasion, Nick?" I let my teeth click on the end of his name. He chuckles darkly as he grabs a goblet from the elf's hand, pouring from the pitcher of mulled wine, sloshing it over the edge as he shoves it my way.

The deep red wine trickles down the side like blood from a festering wound, splashing onto the dark wood table. Nick raises his cup high, and I follow suit. "We have captured another lonely, miserable human, and we're going to break them in tonight. Care to join us? He looks just like your type." He gives me an exaggerated wink.

I chuckle and keep the smile on my face as I hold the goblet to my lips, taking a deep sniff and inhaling the sweet undertone of the mistletoe berries. I pretend to take a sip, then casually raise my glass, showing more of my teeth. "I'm not sure about tonight, Nick. Put me down for an I.O.U."

He grins, and I can tell he thinks I'm unaware of the drugs he's put into the wine; however, he's tricked me one too many times to be fooled again. He loves to spike my drinks, and sometimes, when I can't ignore the twitch of my cock any longer, I dive into it, drinking enough to pass out, hallucinate, and wake up right in the middle of one of his weekly orgies. They've become more frequent lately, and while I appreciate the fun, tonight's just not the night.

"You're no fun anymore, Kryx," he huffs, reaching over and

slapping his hand on my shoulder. "It's been years since you've indulged in any activities in the castle; instead, you hide out in your fortress." His eyes seem to swirl with the darkness that consumes his soul, a flicker of bright blue flames illuminating them. Those same eyes suddenly narrow at me. "Are you hiding a *lover?*" His voice is low, with an accusatory tone. "And you're not *sharing?*"

I laugh at his absurdity. *A lover?*

Nicolette is far from that. However, my obsession with her has led me to take risks over the years, and it's clear that I've been gradually distancing myself from Nick's debauchery. Tonight, though, was different with her. Not only because she was awake and fully aware of my intentions, but the slight pull I've felt in my chest for years was far more vicious than ever before, as if a hook was embedded under my skin, reeling me in and dragging me through the rough waters straight to her.

While she's on the Naughty List, and has been for quite some time, the less he knows about her, the better off we'll all be. If he even suspects that I'm favoring someone, he will undoubtedly drag her here and use her up for himself. And if push came to shove, I would take her to the darkest corners of the South Pole so he could never find her.

Deals be damned.

I give him a dark laugh, once again playing his game. "Only the occasional participant attempting to lighten their sentence." I wink, showing more of my teeth, and make a show of dragging my forked tongue over them. "Which we both know is a lost cause, but it's even more fun for me."

The darkness in his eyes brightens, delight shimmering in his irises. "Good, because that list only keeps growing by the second. Their sins worsen daily, and I don't want you to be distracted. Those mortals deserve every second of their punishments."

He drops back into his seat and notices that Clara has sunk

further into hers, panting as her little pet tongue-fucks her from under the table. He watches, his eyes growing brighter as her pants turn into soft moans, her back arching in her seat. He places his hand over his cock, gripping it as he leans back, taking a long sip of his wine while watching her unravel right here at the table.

Her moans grow louder as she starts to put on a show, and I avert my gaze—I refuse to play into it. She lured me in once, and now they both think I'm a willing participant whenever they want. Clara is a beautiful woman, but her cruelty has begun to rot her from the inside out.

Instead, I think about Nicolette: her curves, her flushed face as she came, and the fact that I didn't repulse her with my confession, and she even asked me to stay. What happened tonight goes against every instinct I have with the job I was assigned to do. I'm supposed to come in, dole out their punishments, and leave.

Unlike tonight, I've never pleasured someone during what they believed was their punishment. Even though her fear was apparent, she wasn't terrified of me, and her pleasure was unmistakable. Usually, the marks I leave on my victims fade, but the bite mark I left tonight will leave a scar, embedding my mark in her skin.

If Nick hadn't been calling on me, would I have listened to her request and stayed? Spent the night as if I were anything more than the demon who had infiltrated her dreams and used her body in every possible way? I can still taste her desire on my tongue and feel the tension in my chest, attempting to pull me right from my chair and back into her bed.

I settle into my seat, making myself comfortable and keeping a smile on my face. As much as I want to leave, I know I have to wait until Nick's drunk enough to slip out quietly; otherwise, he'll throw a fit, and I'll never get the chance to make my escape.

A door opens across the room, and I watch as the elves

march in line, bringing out dishes and sliding them onto the table before removing the lids from the silver platters. It's a small feast of meats, vegetables, winterberry pie, and pastries that will likely go uneaten by us and be secretly consumed later tonight by the other human pets and these little monsters.

I casually set my goblet on the edge of the table, glancing sidelong and nodding as one of the elves grabs it by the stem and sneaks away with it, disappearing through the door that leads to the kitchen. I hate the hideous little bastards, but we've established a system on the nights Nick tries to drug me, so they clear my tainted goblet for a new one, and I let them enjoy the high instead.

Turning my attention back to Nick and Clara, I see they're lost in their pleasure with her human pet, their groans like needles stabbing into my ears. Their chairs scrape loudly across the floor, one of them tipping over with a crash as they move from the table to the large polar bear skin rug near the fire, my presence becoming less important with each passing second.

I wait a few more minutes before I stand, making sure to keep my hooves quiet as I head to the door. I need to get through a few more people on my list before I revisit my little vixen. The demon inside me is itching to show her what I can really do with those whips and chains, and how desperate my shadows are to coil around her. I run my tongue over the roof of my mouth, relishing in the taste of her sweet blood and cum.

As I near the large doors, I glance at the threesome, making sure they're so engrossed in their pleasure that they won't notice my absence. Clara is straddling her human pet's cock, where he lies back on the rug, wrists bound with his arms above his head, a gag over his mouth. Nick stands over him, gripping Clara's hair, and fucks her mouth. He thrusts himself in and out, quietly gagging as she grinds against their pet, their sounds of pleasure blending with the roar of the fire, putting on an erotic show for all their servants who peek out from shadows and hidden doorways.

I smirk at the thought of my little vixen swallowing me whole, tears streaming down her face as I fill her throat with my cum, and my shadows stuffing her full. I let out a quiet groan as I palm my hardening length, the images of her flashing through my mind's eye. If I don't release some of my pent-up energy on the names on my Naughty List, then Nicolette might be in for a bigger world of hurt than she could handle.

She's a criminal—almost a mastermind in her craft of fucking over liars and cheats. Her edges are already jagged; she just needs me to sharpen them even further. I plan to push her until she breaks, and then she'll need me to put her back together.

I turn away as the threesome shifts and changes positions, letting my shadows wrap around me and keep me out of their line of sight. Nick might be distracted at this moment, but he's always watching. He knows more than just when you're sleeping or awake; he also knows your every sin and desire, all just from looking at your name on the list. And he's not afraid to leverage that to get exactly what he wants.

CHAPTER 7

Nicolette

y fingers absentmindedly brush over the teeth marks that mar my skin, letting the pain flicker beneath the surface. I'm still trying to decide if last night was a wet dream or if Krampus himself truly was here, in my cabin, making me come multiple times—if the teeth marks I feel are real or just a hallucination, and I was simply trapped in a lucid dream.

No, Nicolette, the mythical monster, supposedly Santa's right-hand man, was in your cabin last night, had his way with you, and left without saying goodbye or thanks for his orgasm.

Even demons are just like a typical fucking man... except, he didn't just leave, did he? He took the time to care for me. He not only took me to the shower but also ensured I was comfortable, and then sent me off to the most peaceful dreamscape.

There, it was snowy but not cold, and I was surrounded by twinkling lights as I lay on a soft, fur rug in front of an open fire in my plush, floor-length robe. Cardinals fluttered through the air as snowflakes kissed my nose, while the starry sky winked down at me. I could feel him near me, but he was nowhere to be found.

Kryx.

A knot tightens in my chest as tears threaten to spill over, and I blink them away. But he did leave. He showed some decency after tying me to the bed and having his way with me, but that doesn't change what he is: an actual *monster*.

I roll out of bed and yank the sheets off, dried cum splattered across them, and tuck them under my arm. I can still smell him on them, his scent of pine and embers lingering around me, settling into my nostrils.

I step into the living room, expecting it to be freezing since I actually slept all night and didn't tend to the fire like I usually do. Instead, it's warm, the flames burning brightly as if a fresh log had been added. I notice the hoof prints at the edge of the fireplace, and I feel a pang in my chest before it's replaced with fiery rage.

I drop the sheets on the floor and grab the broom to sweep up every bit of soot because how dare he think he can just burst through the door, admit he's been living in my dreams with me for years, make me come harder than I have before, and then just fucking leave.

Fucking bastard.

I lose track of time and rage-clean the entire cabin, and find myself, hours later, standing in the middle of the living room, sweat lingering on my brow and my hair a frizzed mess. I look around and feel my rage turning into embarrassment. I *willingly* let a demon into my fucking bed... and asked him to stay. Like he said, he knocked, and I let him right in. No questions asked.

They've made whole movies about this, and none of them ever seem to end well.

I press my fingers to the tender spot on the inside of my thigh, the pain from the bite now nothing more than a dull ache. Tears burn behind my eyes, and I blink, letting one fall. It burns hot down my cheek before dripping off my chin onto the floor.

Of course, I would be so desperate for attention that I would let the first thing with a dick throw me onto my bed and have their way with me. Pay for the sins of fucking everyone else over by being fucked by one of the ultimate sinners himself. I'm as much of a sucker as the men I prey on.

My pulse races, and a flush of embarrassment spreads up my neck. I shove the cleaning supplies back into the closet, grab my phone and computer, and throw myself down on the couch.

Fuck this shit.

I know I'm supposed to lie low after my last scam, but someone needs to pay for these feelings, and instead of wallowing in them, I'm going to take every penny I can from some very rich, horny man. And it doesn't take long before I get a bite—the dick pics start flowing in, followed by the faceless photos from the models I hired for nude images, serving them up like a catfish dinner.

The storm outside has settled, but another one is approaching, preparing to drop another six to eight inches tonight and tomorrow. That means I won't be going anywhere anytime soon, so I should make the most of my time stuck here. While there's an icy storm outside, there's a firestorm in here, and neither can be stopped.

Mother Nature and Nicolette Evergreen are forces to be reckoned with.

The gloomy daylight quickly fades to black as night settles in, with the wind picking up and becoming violent outside. The fire has yet to die down from whatever magic Kryx used to keep it burning, maintaining the entire cabin at a comfortable warmth and fending off the frigid cold that threatens to seep through the cracks.

He at least left me with something other than an ache in my chest and between my legs.

I mindlessly send message after message, inching closer to closing another deal with a piece of shit who just told me I was more desirable than his wife. I take a screenshot of the message and prepare to send it to her when the time is right, exposing the asshole for who he is. Men like this don't deserve anyone in their lives.

I don't care what kind of person his wife is; no one deserves a cheating partner, and if it's any consolation, I usually send half the money back to their spouses for their troubles. Women supporting women, you know?

My mind starts to drift as the words on the screen blur, replaced by images of last night. Depthless eyes stare down at me, pulling me under like a dark current. Goosebumps spread across my skin as I feel his phantom touch, as if his claws are gently scraping against my skin. My hand slips past the waist-band of my sweatpants, and I imagine his long, forked tongue dragging through my center, flicking my aching clit, making me see stars.

My finger circles around my entrance, my desire dripping and covering my skin. Dragging them up to the sensitive bundle of nerves, I press down, swirling them around as heat builds in my core, threatening to erupt.

I drop my head back against the couch as a small whimper escapes my lips, a moan catching in my throat. My pleasure intensifies as my breathing quickens, along with my own touch. I shift my hips, gaining more access, and an explosion erupts, causing tremors to wrack throughout my body, with bursts of blinding light flashing like fireworks behind my eyelids.

My body relaxes as my hand slips away from between my legs, though I still crave something more. Kryx left me hanging last night, and even though I just got off, I can't seem to find the release I'm looking for. This must be the kind of punishment he intended in my own personal circle of Hell.

The wind outside appears to pick up, rattling the door and threatening to break it down. A gust rushes down the chimney, causing the flames to flare out, licking at the stone hearth. They dance wildly, growing with each gust of the wind, burning through the last threads of my stocking, turning it to ash. My eyes widen as it seems to reach out toward me like a large, clawed hand swiping through the air.

I cry out and press myself back against the couch, curling my knees to my chest. The fiery claws reach out further, their tendrils nearly brushing my skin, the heat warming me even more as I become lost in their movements, letting them hypnotize me.

The cabin slowly fades away, and now I'm standing in a dark cavern, the walls around me glowing bright like molten lava. The shadows swirl as they begin to close in, transforming into long, reaching fingers. I try to make a sound, but nothing comes out as a shadow curls around my neck, tightening its hold and choking all the air from my lungs.

My eyes snap open, and I'm met with familiar, abyssal, hellfire eyes as a large hand grips my throat, holding my head back against the couch, forcing me to look at where Kryx stands behind me. His palm presses against my windpipe just enough to make panic surge and pulse wildly through my veins.

He lowers his face to mine, his large horns curling behind his head like a ram's. His vicious tongue licks his lips, sliding over his piercings, as if he's ready to gobble me up and swallow me whole. "Hello again, little vixen. I see that you started the fun without me." His deep growl rumbles through me as a shadow wraps around my wrist, forcing my hand to reveal my cum-coated fingers.

"*You* weren't invited," I choke out, anger slowly replacing my panic.

His claws prick into my neck, nearly piercing the skin. "*You* don't have the power to make that decision now, not when you continue to be a *very* naughty girl. You manipulated and stole, once again ruining someone's pathetic life, even after I warned you what would happen. And *then* you go and get yourself off to the thought of me." He tsks, harshly clicking his tongue. "Sin, after sin, after *sin*."

My nostrils flare at him as my anger ignites like a match. "Don't be such a conceited asshole," I snap. "It's none of your fucking business who I was getting off to, but it certainly wasn't *you*."

No man or monster controls me, nor does anyone tell me what to do, including this demon. I was raised in a home filled with smoke and mirrors, and I learned far too late not to trust anyone. Those who are supposed to love you most will abandon you in your darkest moments and never look back.

Now, I don't get left; *I* do all the leaving.

Kryx lifts his hand from my throat, allowing me to take a deep breath as he grips my jaw, squeezing my cheeks and puckering my lips. "You may be able to lie to men on the internet, but you will never be able to lie to me, little vixen." He lowers his head further, his nose grazing mine, breathing in deeply. "I can smell your desire. It lingers in the air, coats your fingers thickly, and drips between your legs."

He reaches down with his free hand and pulls mine to his face, the shadow holding it slipping away. He presses my fingers to his lips, his tongue gently caressing them, licking up and down each one. "And it tastes just as delicious as it smells."

"Leave me alone," I grit out through my pursed lips, the words barely escaping my throat as I struggle to suppress a groan. His fingers loosen their grip on my face. "Aren't you supposed to be out fucking other people for their punishments?" I let my anger fuel the fire that rages through my veins, threatening to burn me.

His face stays neutral, but I don't miss the flicker of flames in his eyes. "Do you *want* me to go and fuck someone else, Nicolette?" His voice is a rough whisper, his words sliding along my skin like the edge of a knife. "If that's what you want, then I have an entire list of contenders who will gladly ride my cock for a lesser sentence. I will fill *all* their needy holes with my cum, marking them no differently than I marked you. Will that satisfy you?"

I choke on my retort as the feeling of a phantom fist hitting my chest knocks the words back down my throat. If I say yes, I risk him leaving and doing just what he promised, but if I say no, then I risk him thinking I actually give a fuck about whatever this is, and I need to be the one to stay in control. Instead of answering, I narrow my eyes and reach back, letting my fingers caress the bulge pressing against his black leather pants, feeling each ridge and pulsing vein.

He breathes deeply through his nose; his pupils dilate until they snuff out the fire, and the darkness continues to take over, turning them into nothing more than a depthless void. He drops his hands from me and steps back, putting distance between us as his nostrils flare. Another punch strikes my chest, but I draw the air back into my lungs, refusing to give him any control. Instead of begging him to touch or fuck me, I run my hand down my body and back under the waistband of my joggers.

I keep my eyes on him as I start to touch myself, proving I don't need him or *anyone* else. The darkness spreads from his eyes to his gray skin, resembling roots gripping beneath the surface. "Nicolette," he growls, shaking the floorboards. The veins in his arms turn coal black, pumping inky darkness through his body and creating cracks.

My name is a warning, like a siren calling to take cover from the storm, but I don't listen. He's not the only ruthless monster in the room. I slide my other hand under my sweatshirt, relieved I went the day without a bra, and squeeze my nipple between my fingers and thumb, letting out a quiet gasp.

His body shifts, his hooves scraping against the floorboards as shadows swirl behind him, forming into a massive pair of wings, with a sharp claw curling from the tip. He's terrifying and enigmatic, his eyes flashing bright with fire, and his nostrils flaring. Heat radiates from him, making my body tremble with fear, but I keep going, pushing him even further.

I want to see him come apart—tear me to shreds with his claws and teeth and show me what a demon is really capable of.

Heat flares between my legs, swirling through my abdomen as I speed up my rhythm, pinching my nipple so hard that I whimper. He growls at the sound and palms his growing erection, watching me like a predator watches its prey—a deep hunger in his gaze.

The tension between us is electric, sending a crackle of lightning between my legs. I press my fingers firmly to my clit and pinch my nipple, shutting my eyes tight. I tumble over the edge, crying out as a wave of pleasure overtakes me, the sound echoing throughout the cabin, bouncing wildly off the walls, until it falls silent.

My eyes flutter open, and I lift my head to look around—or at least try to. The fire is out, and the room is shrouded in darkness. My heart pounds as I shift on the couch, leaning forward, with the wood supports creaking beneath me. I blink, trying to adjust my eyes—but it feels as if I'm wearing a blindfold.

I sit up just as Kryx's voice fills the room, his words low and breathy, his intentions loud and clear. "Oh, Nicolette, you're such a naughty girl who has no idea what kind of trouble she's gotten herself into." I shift on the couch and look behind me, trying to locate him in the dark to no avail. A floorboard creaks, and I turn my head just as I feel claws scrape across my scalp, his hand plunging into my hair.

He yanks me off the couch and onto my knees, darkness lifting as his eyes burn bright. "And now, little vixen, I'm going to show you your *real* punishment."

CHAPTER 8

Kryx

Nicolette crossed a fucking line, and now it's time for this little vixen to see exactly what the Devil of Christmas can *really* do. Earlier was merely a jolly good time, but now it's time for her to find out what punishments I have up my sleeves—punishments as dark as the blood that courses through my veins.

If she thinks I spent years watching her—*waiting* for her—just for last night to be the only night I get to sink my teeth into her, then she's sorely mistaken.

And she *will* be sore from her mistake.

I stare down at her flushed face, letting my claws dig into her scalp while I grip her thick, curly, red hair tightly. She's panting, trembling—her desire's scent mixing with her fear, swirling around me, nipping at me more than the frigid wind howling outside.

"W-what are you going to do to me?" she whimpers as I tilt her head back further, exposing her throat and watching her pulse pound against her delicate, porcelain skin. The faint tremor of fear in her words is the sweetest sound, making me even harder as she shudders out a shallow breath. She's strong and defiant, but I love nothing more than watching her fall to her knees and hearing her desperate pleas.

Why tell her when I can fucking *show* her?

My shadows snake out from under the sofa and curl over the edge of the cushion. They grip the front of her sweatshirt, tearing it open and exposing her bare chest, then slide the shredded fabric down and off her arms. "Hey, you fuckin—" Her words are cut off as a shadow curls over her mouth and muffles her words. Her eyes widen with panic as more shadows tear away her pants, leaving them as nothing more than rags on the floor and exposing her curves and the bite mark I gifted her last night.

"Mm, no underwear in sight, you *naughty* girl," I croon as I reach down and slide a claw down her throat, feeling the vibrations of her muffled pleas as I grip her chin, running my thumb across her jaw.

Shadows slither across the floor, rising like snakes, ready to strike, before they coil around her wrists, yanking them behind her back and binding them together in one fell swoop. She lets out a muffled cry, her fear intensifying—the smell of it permeating the room and coating my skin like a warm winter coat.

My shadows curl behind her head, wrapping around and hooking the sides of her mouth, forcing it open while the other falls to her shoulders and brushes across her collarbone. She whimpers as I slowly undo the laces on my pants, my cock springing free just inches from her panic-stricken face. Her eyes are wide as the fire I snuffed out rekindles, the crackling embers roaring to life and warming the room.

Her red hair gleams against the golden rings wrapped around my fingers, her freckles like a dusting of stars across her cheeks and nose. Her green eyes sparkle like glittering lights as tears well up at the corners from the tight grip as I hold on to her hair.

She's fucking stunning.

"Stick out your tongue, little vixen, and you'll have a front row seat to how I fully intend to punish you," I say, a growl rumbling at the back of my throat.

She whimpers and squeezes her legs together as if her pussy isn't already dripping for me. I smirk as more shadows curl around her thighs, shifting her knees and forcing her legs apart. "I expect a mess on the floor from your tight, needy cunt." With my free hand on my length, I pump it up and down, spreading my precum down my shaft. "Now stick out your fucking tongue before I yank it out," I growl, the darkness seeping into the veins around my eyes, revealing another glimpse of my monstrous side.

Her brows shoot up in surprise, but she tentatively sticks out her tongue, saliva gathering on it and threatening to drip down her chin. I pray to Satan himself that she'll be covered in it by the time I'm done shamelessly fucking her mouth—giving me a reason to slide my aching cock between her full, perky breasts.

Gripping the base, I rest the tip of my length onto her awaiting tongue and rock my hips back and forth, coating myself and forcing the spit to cascade down onto her chest. My shadows pull her mouth farther open, stretching her lips and giving me easier access. My cock presses against it, and she quietly gags as I hold her head steady and increase my speed, pushing myself deeper into her tight throat with each thrust.

"*Fuck,*" I grit out. "This mouth is the gift I've waited all year for." I thrust with every word, and she moans, the sound vibrating through me, and if I'm not careful, I'll be coming like a fucking virgin.

She moans again as I pick up the pace, drool running down her chin and onto her chest like a melting icicle. I groan, the sound nearly a growl, as I watch the light from the fireplace flicker across her wet skin, my balls tightening in warning. I pull back, releasing her hair as she sucks in a deep breath, pushing her breasts out, her chest quickly rising and falling. Her eyes drift toward the corners of her mouth, waiting for the shadows to release her, but instead, one curls past her open lips and disappears behind her teeth.

Her eyes widen with panic before they suddenly blaze with fury, her silence so loud that it seems to rattle the windows more than any blizzard ever could. Her jaw tightens, her teeth grinding into the shadow as I lean down and grip her chin. A claw from my free hand traces across her throat, leaving a red streak and raising goosebumps.

"Look at what the devil does to you, you naughty thing." My grin widens as more shadows wrap around her ankles, anchoring her in place. "Baby, it's cold outside, but hot as hell in here."

I can't help but chuckle as she tries to curse me around the shadow stuffed in her mouth, puffing out her cheeks as if she's a chipmunk. She's not just a lump of hot coal; she's a blazing hell-fire—heating me to my core. Her fiery red hair shines as a sign of her devilishness and how careful I should be if I want to avoid getting burned. But as a demon from Hell, I fucking love the flames.

My shadows keep her in place as the quiet rattling of chains fills the air, and her body stiffens while her gaze darts around the room. They wrap around her legs, cross her chest, and coil around her delicate neck, linking together into a metal collar. The remaining length extends to where I hold out my hand, the cool metal resting against my palm as I curl my fingers around it.

I give the chain a gentle tug, watching it jerk her forward, her eyes widening again as she lets out a muffled yelp. My thick cock twitches as I look down at her, and I grip the base, sliding my hand up and down my length. She stares up at me, and where there should be fear, there's only fury, as if the moment I release her, she'll pounce and tear me limb from limb.

She would look extraordinary standing over me, splattered

in my blood as I take my final breath, my still-beating heart in her hands.

"My pretty little pet," I growl, a slight tingle dancing at the base of my spine. "I love seeing you on your knees, and even more, I love the look of defiance on your face as you play the part of the fucking *brat*." She exhales sharply through her nostrils, her jaw ticking, and I let out a scoff of laughter. "We'll see how far you can bend before you finally break."

I snap my fingers, and we're transported into her bedroom, where she's ass-up on the bed, her arms under her body with her wrists tied to her ankles. The chain that collars her throat is wrapped around the footboard of the bed, keeping her in place —exactly where I want her. I kick the door shut behind me, the wooden doorframe rattling as I take a long step forward and examine her.

"Look at you," I say with a fiendish smile. "All wrapped up like the perfect present, just waiting for me to tear open."

Her pale skin is flushed, and her hair is wild, the curls springing against the mattress. Her full hips and ass are just begging for me to sink my teeth into them. The chain clinks quietly, mimicking the sound of sleigh bells as she shifts on the bed, her breath sharp through her nose. The scent of her desire gradually fills the room, like smoke from a fire, replacing the air in my lungs with a sweet, intoxicating aroma.

Whether she remembers or not, she's always wanted me.

Begs for me every chance she gets.

But even as my cock aches for her, watching her squirm as she searches for release, she remains my forbidden fruit. My shadows and chains might bind her, filling her, letting her taste my cock as I come down her throat, or taste her cum as it drips off my fingertips, but there's a line I can't cross, no matter how desperately I want to. The pull I feel to her is tighter than any knot I could make and threatens to choke the life out of me if I'm not careful.

She's at war with her own desires as my shadows tease her clit and ass, while another slowly pumps in and out of her dripping pussy. I curl my hand into a loose fist and feel the smooth handle of the flogger as it appears in my palm, the soft, leather tendrils falling over my fingers. I move to the side, placing myself directly in her line of sight. She instantly tenses up as her eyes fix on my favorite toy, her whimpers of desperation vibrating in her throat.

The thin strips of leather glide across her skin, goosebumps rising as I slide my hand under her cheek to cup her face and gently turn her glassy eyes to me. "You burn as bright as the hellfire that kindles in my soul," I say lowly. "And I welcome the flame that licks at me and chars my skin like an old friend. A *lover*."

Pulling my hand away, I drag the flogger along her spine, letting it fan out over her ass before flicking my wrist. The sound of the leather cracking fills the silence, leaving red marks that mar her delicate skin. She lets out a deep, guttural moan, and I can't help but chuckle.

"You love the pain, don't you, little vixen?" I ask as I flick my wrist again, bringing the tendrils across her backside, where she lets out a muffled scream. "You are something so wild that no matter how hard anyone tries, you can never be tamed."

And I never want you to be.

I slide my hand between her legs, and my shadows pull back, exposing her glistening pussy. "You're going to come all over my hand, and when you do, then it's my turn. And I'm going to cover you in my cum and mark you as *mine*." She moans again as I slide my fingers through her slit, pressing my middle finger against her entrance, teasing her. "I want to hear you scream my name," I growl as I release the shadow that was gagging her.

She sucks in a deep breath, her ribs expanding as her pussy clenches around my finger. "You're a fucking *monster*," she gasps, almost choking on the words.

I lean down as I add another digit, continuing to pump my fingers slowly in and out, letting my pointer finger glide over her swollen clit. "And yet, you have never tried to stop me. It's as if you're *enjoying* yourself." I halt my movements, and she whimpers, her desire soaking into my skin and fusing to my bones. "It's almost as if you've finally met your monstrous match."

"*Kryx*," she moans, as if she's sending up a prayer to the god who never listens, but knows the devil beside her will *always* answer her pleas.

"Nicolette," I growl as I whip the flogger against her backside again and again, her cries echoing through the room, sending her soaring. "*Come. For. Me.*" The strips of leather hit her skin with every word.

I bring the flogger down once again, pressing my finger against her clit as she screams my name. Her inner walls contract, and her cum floods my cupped hand. Wave after wave of pleasure crashes over her, burying her—drowning her. I draw out the tide as long as possible, regretting not having her mounted on my face and drinking her dry.

I drag my hand away and bring it to my lips, where it glistens in the light. I glide my tongue over my fingers, the taste of her exploding in my mouth, and I can't help but moan. I continue to suck on them as I let the flogger fall to the floor, my now-free hand gripping my length and giving it a rough jerk.

My eyes flicker down, and I see her watching me; her normally fury-filled eyes are hypnotic as desire swirls through them. She stares at my cock, licking her lips as precum drips onto the floor. The air turns thick as she pulls against her bindings, attempting to break free as her own cum slides down her inner thighs.

I want to pound into her needy cunt, press my claws into her delicate skin, and leave more of my marks all over her body—make her *mine*. The need for her is too much as my vision blurs and a tingle ignites at the base of my spine, spreading like hellfire to my cock. My monstrous side breaks free as I jerk my fingers from my mouth and reach down to grip her hair. Yanking her across the bed, I leave her no time to react as I come all over her full, pouty lips.

I roar, my head falling back as my orgasm racks through me, nearly sending me to my knees. I squeeze my length until every last drop is speckled across her face, concealing her freckles. I huff in a shuddering breath and take in the mess I've made of her. My fingers are tangled in her mane, and I watch as she drags her tongue across her lips and moans.

Goddammit.

I smirk as I smear my fingers across her cheek, coating them in my cum, and stuffing the digits into her mouth. She roughly sucks on them, and I feel my cock harden again so quickly that it has me seeing stars. Hell only knows how I relish in the pain.

"So fucking *naughty*," I croon, pressing my fingers against the back of her throat, where she lets out a quiet gag, her throat flexing around my digits. "And just think, I've only just started to collect for the long list of sins you've committed. This could take *all night*."

Her eyes widen as I lift my other hand and snap my fingers, plunging the room into complete darkness.

CHAPTER 9

Kryx

My shadows slip away from Nicolette's unmoving body, where she lies sprawled out on the bed, covered in cum and red marks. Her eyes flicker beneath her lids as her chest slowly rises and falls, her mind lost in a dreamlike state as she sinks deeper into sleep. I watch her from the end of the bed, my eyes glued to the swell of her breasts, my fingers itching to touch her—fuck her all over again.

Although I might have been the one to bind and shackle her, she has taken control of my mind and imprisoned me with thoughts I've never experienced for anyone else. She should fear me, but the fiery look in her eyes says otherwise. I am a powerful demon, capable of destruction beyond any mortal's comprehension, and yet, I would fall to my knees for this woman and worship her at any altar.

A resplendent fallen angel.

I watch as the corners of her mouth curl up into a ghost of a smile that makes me wonder what she's seeing... *who* she's seeing.

I'm the one who sent her to her dreamscape, and while I would usually let my curiosity get the best of me and take a look, I've done enough damage for tonight. There will be plenty of opportunities to cross into her unprotected mind, but for now, I must continue with my duties and check off the names that have been plaguing my list for too long. I don't want Nick to think I'm going soft—or getting distracted.

I take a slow step back, my body yearning to slip into the sheets and curl around her, but I resist. I reach behind me and turn the handle, keeping my eyes on her sleeping form and being careful not to let my hooves make too much noise on the hard floors as I finally make my exit to the living room, leaving her bedroom door cracked. I stare into the fireplace, checking that the piece of coal I left is still nestled in the embers, its magic keeping the fire blazing hot and heating the entire cabin.

I look back over my shoulder and stare at Nicolette's figure, outlined in red from the flames of her wood burner. A small voice in my mind urges me to turn on a hoof and hide in this blizzard with her. But the other, more rational voice booms over it, telling me to go back to the North Pole and keep Nick off her scent and out of my business. If he catches sight of a wretched soul around Christmas, they might find themselves swept away to Santa's Castle, never to be seen again.

And while Nicolette chooses to be alone, she's at the top of the Naughty List and has been inching her way up for a long time, unknowingly on the Clauses' radar. I've managed to keep them off her scent so far, and I'll make sure she remains just a name—one that's clearly crossed off. She would be a prize for them with her stunning curves and full breasts, along with her perfect pussy. And most importantly, she's a complete fucking brat.

My fucking brat.

The Clauses are dangerous and willing to cross boundaries to get what they want or who they want. Nicolette has been mine longer than she realizes, and I plan to keep her for me and *only* me. If those sadistic fucks so much as lay a finger on her, they'll find out what my whips and chains are *really* capable of.

Fortunately, the snow will keep her confined for a few more days until the stormy weather settles, and we can safely get her out. Until then, I will keep her warm by the fire every night and take the liberty of adding her to my personal Naughty List. We have a lot of catching up to do.

I force myself to turn away, pulling my shadows back from where they wait at her bedroom door. Staring intensely into the flames, I take a deep breath, causing the embers to float up and swirl around me, opening the portal that leads directly to the North Pole.

I step forward, my hooves sinking into the deep snow as another storm whips through, large flakes pelting my face. I look up at Nick's castle, my heart thundering in my chest, as I take in the dark, rolling clouds and lightning flashing on the horizon. I shift my gaze to the perimeter and see that not a single elf or reindeer is in sight, which can only mean he's either on a warpath or has an undesirable guest lurking on the grounds.

Fucking fantastic.

The heavy doors swing open as I approach, quickly shutting behind me once I'm inside and cutting off the raging storm. The corridor is dark, and the candles that normally burn brightly are dim, casting ominous shadows on the walls. Something feels off and has me on edge.

Here, I usually don't bother to keep my hooves quiet, letting Nick know of my presence, but tonight feels different. The air is thick with tension as I move toward the throne room, my shadows spreading out like enormous wings behind me. The doors are closed, but the flickering light on the other side seeps through the cracks, bleeding out on the stone floor. I place my hand on the heavy iron pull, hesitating as I hear low voices on the other side—one that sends a shiver up my spine.

Jack Frost.

That motherfucker is the root of everyone's problems and would have been better off lost in the same snowy haze as the rest of the humans they harbor here. Jack was once only a favored pet of Clara and Nick. Still, he somehow managed to manipulate them and convince them to strike a deal that not only granted him immortality but also gave him the powers of a guardian, allowing him to serve them in more ways than one. They made him out to be their assistant to deal with the monsters that dwell among the snowdrifts and help in other frigid parts of the world. But in reality, he's nothing more than their icy spy, causing chaos wherever he goes.

His presence explains the ominous weather outside and why there aren't any elves or reindeer around. While they're vile creatures, he's an even bigger sadist than any of us, and they don't want to get caught in his icy torture. Still, I quickly scan the hall for the little snitches before pressing my ear to the door, while my shadows curl around me in an attempt to catch any words slipping through the cracks.

"You're a fool if you believe what that demon tells you, Nicholas," Jack says inside the chamber, his voice clear and firm. I hold my breath, trying to calm the anxiety that pinches at my skin.

Has he been spying on me?

Nick lets out a boisterous laugh, echoed by the soft clink of his goblet against the table. "Oh, come now, Jack, let her have her fun. She will get bored soon and return to her regular duties of hunting and killing, while keeping the mountainfolk in line."

I let out a breath of relief, my warm breath curling through the air. The little fucking rat has been off stalking other demons across the globe, and not only reporting back, but also snitching on them. He's heinous and harbors a deep loathing for the connection between Nick and me, which neither of us can control. I spent years putting up walls to keep Nick out, and I doubled down when he granted Jack guardianship.

Though I technically hold a higher rank in Hell than Nick, he wields more power on Earth and has declared himself king of this realm—a king I would never kneel to. While I am extremely powerful, I'm not foolish enough to challenge him. Even if I were to win, there would be too many out for my blood to usurp his icy throne—one I have no desire for—and bear his gilded holly crown.

I straighten my spine and pull back my shadows, their tendrils fluttering behind me. I intend to not only intimidate the little fuck, but also remind him that he doesn't hold a candle to me or my power. He believes he has the upper hand because he submits to Nick and Clara, fulfilling all their desires. In reality, he's nothing more than their little fuck toy—his title doesn't mean shit.

Yanking the door open, their heads snap in my direction, and I make a grand entrance. The veins in my arms throb black, stretching across my body, blending into the tattoos inked across my chest, and my eyes glow as red as the twinkling lights that decorate the evergreen towering in the corner. My shadows swirl around me like the wings of a fallen angel, with the tips trailing behind like a cape. My hooves click loudly on the stone, echoing through the room and making Jack wince with every step. I let my élan crackle like an eternal flame, a reminder to everyone in the room who truly is the most powerful being in the North Pole.

Nick blinks slowly before spreading his arms wide, obviously intoxicated on his winterberry wine, and shouts my name in his cheerful Santa voice. "Kryx, I was hoping like a child on Christmas Eve you would come tonight."

Jack's icy blue eyes darken as he looks me up and down, his snow-white skin turning a bitter blue as his face flushes, with his snow-blown hair falling over his forehead. I hold his gaze as his bitter draft presses against my shadows, trying to disrupt them and expose my back. The tension in the room grows as the storm rages outside, but Nick doesn't even seem to notice.

"Jack, you remember Kryx?" he says as he slaps him hard on the back, jolting him forward and nearly knocking him off his feet.

I can't stop the grin that pulls up my lips, revealing my sharp teeth. Of course, he remembers me. One doesn't simply forget the demon you've relentlessly followed around like a half-frozen puppy in an attempt to fuck them and make your handlers jealous.

"Hello, Jack," I say slyly, giving him a wink and running my tongue over my exposed teeth.

His blue eyes swirl with ire as a draft drifts into the room, dropping the temperature a few bitter degrees. "*Krampus*," he bites, attempting to use the word as an insult.

Krampus is simply the persona that humanity created for me —a stern warning to those who find themselves on my list. It's nothing more than the name they desperately beg for mercy with, pleading on their knees as I deliver their punishments. The celebrity status fuels my powers, giving me access to their minds and free rein over their hopes, dreams, and *fears*.

It's just like how Nick's Santa Claus persona fuels him with the joy from his loyal believers during the holiday season, giving him powers that last all year.

This is what sets Nick and me apart, elevating us above Jack, who is merely a trickster using his cold and snow as smoke and mirrors. He might think he's a force to be reckoned with here, scaring the lesser beings, but he's nothing more than a few warm holes for Nick and Clara to use as they please. Regardless, he always has something up his sleeve, and if my suspicions are correct—based on the snippet of conversation I overheard—he's here to do more than just get on his knees for his weekly fucking.

Nick holds out a second goblet, filled to the brim with deep maroon wine, a dribble sloshing over the edge. Curling my fingers around it, I politely take it, shifting my attention to him and giving him a smile that would terrify any human—except maybe Nicolette. My little vixen stared down her nose at this very grin and held her gaze, seeming to count every tooth on display.

"What brings you here two nights in a row, Kryx?" he asks merrily over the rim of his cup, maroon liquid dripping onto his white beard, staining the strands crimson. "While I always anticipate your arrival, this is a rare occurrence."

I don't miss the way Jack cocks his head to the side and narrows his brows at me. It's unusual for me to make an appearance at the castle two nights in a row, since I usually try to make my list and check it twice, so I don't have to come back often. Still, I don't let his noticing of my behavior shake my answer, even as my heart races.

"Well, Nick," I begin, my mouth wide in a smile similar to his. "It *is* getting close to Christmas, you know? And I'm just checking to see if there are any additions to the ever-growing Naughty List that I might need to prioritize. As much as you feed off the joy, I also know you *love* the chance to ruin someone's holiday season."

He laughs, breaking the small bubble of tension that was hanging in the room and putting me at ease. "Oh, yes, there's a handful of them that need to be left begging for mercy. Let me grab my list from the study and give you an update." He grabs my shoulder, stumbling slightly as he passes.

With him gone, I'm left alone with Jack, whose gaze burns into me—frostbite personified. "You know," I say as my shadows tighten around me, deflecting his chill, "if you pump him with too many mistletoe berries, he won't be able to fuck you." My lips curl into a wicked grin as frost creeps across the floor, trying to gather around my hooves, but my shadows keep it at bay.

"*You* would know, wouldn't you?" he retorts, squaring his shoulders as he drinks from his own goblet.

The jealous little bastard always reveals his cards when it comes to Nick. It's comical, the idea of Nick being more than two parts of one of Lucifer's bargains. We have turned to dust long before I would ever fall into bed with him. I've participated in his orgies for centuries, where we both have gained quite a reputation, but I've never let Nick take things too far, no matter how ruthlessly he tries.

However, I love seeing the vengeful little icicle steam as Nick rests a hand on my shoulder, or as his fingers brush mine in the passing of a goblet. I enjoy engaging in the constant flirting and watching as he desperately throws himself at Nick's feet, trying to divert his attention.

Torture is my drug of choice and one I so gleefully dole out, especially to the pathetic little snowball.

"Has he ever told you what his favorite position is?" I ask coolly as I lower myself into one of the chairs already pulled out at the banquet table.

"Don't be so brazen," he says sharply. "It's doggie style, with him on top."

He watches me, his brow quirking slightly as I pick up one of the already-poured goblets and give it a tentative sniff. I let out an approving grunt before swallowing it in one gulp, slamming the now-empty cup back onto the table. I can't help but smirk because even a stranger would know that about him just by looking at the fucker.

"What's his favorite way to be dominated?" I ask, tracing my claw along the rim of the cup, collecting a drop that I bring up and let fall to my tongue.

He freezes, his eyes narrowing as my gaze flickers back to

him, raising an eyebrow. "He doesn't like to be dominated," he retorts. His words are tight as he forces them out through his gritted teeth, his fingers curling into a fist around the stem of his cup.

Snorting a laugh, I look toward the doors just as Nick reenters, holding his list above his head and waving it like a flag. "If you say so," I say lowly, just loud enough for Jack to hear, making his face turn even bluer with rage.

I stand, shoving the chair back and holding out my hand just as Nick slaps the list onto my palm. "I think you'll find your victims to be fun tonight, Kryx," he says right before he downs another goblet of wine, swaying on his feet, a hiccup pulsing past his lips.

I make a show of holding up the list with both hands, studying the names of my victims, with one jumping out at me, almost taking my breath away.

Evelyn Evergreen.

The name is written neatly at the top of the list. I glance at the parchment as Nick leans over the table, reaching for the half-empty pitcher of wine. Jack lunges forward, catching it just before it slips from his fingers. I quickly scan the list and notice Nicolette's name is no longer there.

Thank fuck.

I glance up at Nick, letting my mouth split into a nightmarish grin, my sharp teeth flashing. "Tonight will be one for the books," I chuckle, my throat drying as I fold up the list and slide it into my pocket. "Don't wait up," I wink, causing Nick to throw his head back and laugh, completely throwing him off balance. He falls on his ass, his hiccupped laugh only growing louder as Jack tries to pull him back to his feet.

I use the chaos to slip away and move into the corridor, my eyes catching on someone standing silently in the shadows, their cold gaze burning into me. But I don't look back as I dash down the hall and out into the raging storm.

The sooner I get through this wretched list and figure out how to handle the name at the very top, the sooner I can get back to my little vixen.

CHAPTER 10

12 YEARS EARLIER

Kryx

I steady my feet, my hooves quietly scraping on the shingles as I stand on the rooftop, claws gripping the edge of the dormer. The house is silent, and the only light is the glow of the Christmas tree in the front window, which illuminates the house. It's nearly one o'clock in the morning, and if I'm correct, it's due to turn off at any moment, plunging the house into complete darkness.

The drapes in the window have been left open, allowing the moonlight to make the long hallway glow brightly. The room of my target is three doors down, but her scent is too faint for her to be on this floor, which means she must be sleeping somewhere else in the house. I slowly turn, being careful not to make a noise, when I notice a subtle movement out of the corner of my eye.

The faint scent of vanilla and shea butter fills my nostrils, stopping me dead in my tracks. A knot tightens in my chest, trying to steal my breath. I carefully move closer to the window and crouch down, catching the silhouette of a woman as she unhurriedly shuffles down the hall in her gray robe and slippers. The wind blows against my back, pushing me forward; my hand rises to brace against the window, causing my claws to tap against the glass and produce a loud pop in this nearly silent night.

The woman freezes, her robe fluttering as she comes to a halt, and I suck in a sharp breath, my heart rattling my ribs. Her red curls are a wild mane as she slowly turns her head, her piercing green eyes flashing while she stares back at me. But to her, I am nothing more than a dark cloud blocking the moon, with shadows curling around me like a cocoon, hiding me from sight. She turns back toward the other end of the hall just as the Christmas tree lights go out, plunging the house into darkness —exactly as I planned.

She stands silently for a moment before huffing a deep sigh, crossing her arms over her chest, shaking her head slowly, then turning on her heel and shuffling back through the door she came through, closing it behind her with a quiet click. I count to ten, letting the house settle again, then carefully lift the window and let the cold wind rush in, pulling me inside.

I stand guard as the window quietly slides shut behind me, and the house warms as heat blows from the register. My hooves sink into the plush rug that stretches through the hall as I take a tentative step forward, staying concealed in my shadowy shroud as I pass the door she disappeared through. Her intoxicating scent floods my senses, making my mouth water as I turn toward the closed door. I lean forward, gripping the doorframe as I press my ear against the smooth wood.

I hear the mattress creak, along with the shuffle of the sheets, as she tucks herself back in. There's murmuring, her voice thick with sleep as she lets out a long, exasperated breath.

Is she talking to someone?

Is there someone else in there with her?

It's crucial that I know how many people are here and their whereabouts, to avoid getting caught or disrupting my work, especially since there was only supposed to be one person here tonight. I press my ear harder against the wood, but now there's only heavy silence on the other side. My fingers twitch as my hand hovers over the doorknob, but I force it away, almost stumbling back as I fight the urge to burst into her room and claim her—punish her.

What the fuck is wrong with me?

My number one rule is not to interfere with people who aren't on my list, let alone walk into their fucking rooms and interrupt their slumber. The last few times I've been to this house, I've never encountered another woman here, and certainly not her.

I would fucking remember.

I'm a monster—a demon—and the stories of Krampus have been twisted over the centuries, making me out to be a thief in the night, kidnapping children and whipping them. And while I'll occasionally encounter innocent children who have woken up and crawled out of their warm beds, they're not who I'm after. I'm after the true terrors of this world—*adults*.

However, there's no kidnapping involved. I simply slip into their dreams and hunt them through their dreamscapes. My instincts make me hellbent on leaving behind marks for when they wake, a reminder that if they keep up their naughty habits, I'll be back until they finally learn their lesson—if they ever do.

I hear the mattress creak again, my body thrumming with anticipation. This woman, nestled in her bed, sends a curling heat through me—one that intensifies with each passing second.

Who the fuck is she?

My hand drifts back to the handle, my instincts pleading with me to go inside as my heart pounds against my ribs. I curl my fingers around the brass, my hand warming the metal. My grip is so tight that it almost begins to melt beneath my palm. My instincts surge forward, grabbing hold of me by my horns, and just as I start to turn it, the grandfather clock chimes below. Each chime pulls me back to reality while snuffing out the fire that was beginning to burn me from the inside out.

I take a long step back from the door, shake my head, and shove away the impulsive thoughts racing through my mind. I run my hand through my hair, pushing it back from my face, and take another steadying breath. If I didn't know better, I'd think this woman was a witch who had cast a spell on me and was waiting for me to fall into her trap.

Get your shit together, Kryx.

I turn and creep down the hall, stopping at the top of the stairs. My hand rests on the banister as my eyes scan the living room, landing on the figure stretched out on the couch, covered with a throw blanket that hides their face—but it's no use. I know exactly who they are.

I take a deep breath, and the smell of strawberries fills my nose—the very scent I was looking for when I arrived. My shadows cover me as I slip down the stairs, and in a blink, I find myself behind the couch, watching as the woman takes deep breaths, drifting deeper into her sweet dreams.

I hear a quiet click near the fireplace, as if the flue is being closed. My gaze snaps up, and I stand as still as a deer in the forest, watching for whoever else might be lurking in the shadows. I half-expect a cat to come out from under the tree, but it's as if whatever was there has vanished into the night.

I lean in and listen, but the only sound is the ticking of the grandfather clock, a reminder of the seconds I'm wasting in this wretched house. I look over the woman's delicate body, the blanket tucked tightly around her, as if she were lying down for a long winter's nap. Even after checking the list twice, I'm still unsure of this woman's crimes or why I need to impose one of my strictest punishments, but the list knows, and I don't question it.

In fact, this isn't the first time I've been to this house, face to face with the woman who's always asleep on the couch. My arrival is timed just before the tree lights go out, and I feel like she's waiting for Santa Claus himself. But I'm clearly reading too much into this, and it's only a coincidence.

I scan the room one last time before my shadows spread out behind me like mighty wings, filling the space and plunging me deep into the woman's dreams, where it doesn't take long to find her and deliver the punishment she's destined to endure.

I step out of the woman's mind, my hooves softly clicking against the floor. Although it feels like hours in her dreamscape, only minutes have passed in the real world. Her cries of mercy and pleas for forgiveness echo in my ears as I examine her, noticing the trickle of blood at the corner of her mouth and her skin covered in a sheen of sweat.

This punishment better stick, for goodness' sake, because I don't know how much more this woman can handle before she finally breaks. Her eyes were cloudy, and her face nearly sallow as I led her to the pillory, tears streaking her cheeks as she faced her punishment head-on. Whatever she's done seems unforgivable and is slowly eating away at her.

I almost feel concerned for her, but as Krampus, caring isn't part of my role. The people I visit must pay for their crimes eventually, and she is no exception.

I step away from the woman, moving back toward the stairs to make space for my portal to the North Pole, when I hear footsteps coming from upstairs. I glance around as my shadows wrap around me and slip into a dark hallway—out of sight.

The woman from earlier descends the stairs, her brows knit together as she approaches the couch. "Mom?" she whispers, her voice roughened with sleep as she reaches over the back, shaking the woman's shoulder. "It's time to put you to bed. Okay?"

The woman on the couch groans as she rolls over, looking up at the younger woman who seems to have stolen the air from the room. "Nikki," the woman groans breathlessly. "I had that nightmare again. It seemed so real."

Nikki.

"It was just a dream," Nikki says as she slides the blanket off her mother and carefully folds it over the back of the couch. "Come on. Let's go upstairs."

"But," the woman says, tears welling in her eyes as her gaze shifts to the fireplace, "I can't leave yet."

Nikki's gaze softens as it shifts to the cold, empty hearth. "There are still ten days until Christmas, Mom. And we're both a little too old to believe in Santa, aren't we?"

I watch as she extends her hand, urging her mother away from the couch and guiding her back up the stairs, but just as they reach the halfway point, Nikki pauses. Her gaze shifts across the fireplace and fixes on the dark corner where I stand, stone-still. Her brows crease as her eyes narrow, trying to peer into the darkness as if she knows I'm here—my pounding heart threatening to give me away.

"Nikki, is everything okay?" her mother asks, drawing her attention away from me.

"Uh, yeah," she replies, swallowing thickly. "I just thought I saw something."

Her mother chuckles, curling her fingers even tighter around the railing. "It's probably nothing more than a Christmas mouse scurrying through."

"You're right," Nikki replies softly, tightening her hold on her mother's arm. "I'm obviously still half asleep and my mind's playing tricks on me."

They continue their ascent and disappear beyond the landing, where I wait in silence until I hear that they're both back in bed, and the house settles into silence again. My shadows fall away, trailing down my back like a cloak as I step into the living room. I scan the room and approach the fireplace, breathing in the sweet scent of peppermint I hadn't noticed before.

How odd.

I swipe my finger across the hearth, soot covering the surface, and look at it curiously—this fireplace is gas, not wood-burning. *What the hell?* I bend over to investigate the hearth when the grandfather clock chimes softly behind me, breaking the heavy silence in the room and halting my racing thoughts.

"*Shit*," I murmur as I step back and check the time. I've let myself get too wrapped up in this and need to move the fuck on. I look up the stairs, imagining Nikki sound asleep with visions of sugarplums dancing in her head, as I cup my palm, filling it with my signature sparkling sand.

I open my palm and blow across it, letting the dust drift through the air, my shadows whisking it up the stairs, where it will slip under the door and land in the corners of Nikki's eyes —sending her off to a dreamscape I've curated just for her.

CHAPTER 11

Nicolette

My sugarplum dreams darken, shifting like Kryx's shadows, and my skin prickles, the hairs rising on my nape. I step out of the darkness and find myself in the middle of the living room of my childhood home, where Christmas lights twinkle, casting a warm glow. I hear a quiet creak above me and turn to face the stairs, as the sound of boots thumping the ceiling grows louder.

"Hello," I call, the word echoing through the house. "Who's there?"

The footsteps stop suddenly as I try to take a step forward, the floor giving way beneath me, and the dark abyss pulling me under. I attempt to scream, but it's nothing more than a choked cough. I cling to the edge, my nails cracking as I claw at the floor, the wood splintering. My legs swing wildly below me, desperately searching for something solid to push against, but there's only frigid air wrapping around my ankles like weights. My palms slip, and just as I'm about to fall, a large, black tipped hand grabs my wrist and pulls me up.

Strong arms wrap around me, nearly smothering me as I'm pressed against a hard chest, the smell of embers and pine filling my nostrils. A deep voice rumbles through the room, rattling me awake as they say, "*Wake up, little vixen.*"

My eyes flutter open, and I find myself in darkness as a tall figure stands beside the bed, casting a shadow over me and blocking the glow of the fire crackling behind them. I try to sit up, but Kryx's hand wraps around my throat, pinning me to the bed and squeezing the air out of my lungs.

Clawing at his arms, I try to loosen his grip, but he doesn't budge. His eyes flash like raging hellfire as he watches me squirm in his hold, heat flooding between my legs as my desire mixes with fear—adrenaline pulsing through me, straight to my core. His claws prick my skin as I struggle against them until they finally slice through, the metallic scent of my blood swirling through the air.

His eyes widen as the scent hits him, and his nostrils flare while he leans forward, just inches from my face, taking a slow, deep breath. "You smell *divine*, Nicolette," he growls, like a starved animal. "The mix of your blood and arousal is making my mouth water. The beast within me is nearly starved." His teeth flash in the firelight, looking even sharper and longer than before. "I could devour you whole, right *here*, right *now*."

His long tongue slips from between his lips, flicking across his knuckles and tickling my skin. He groans even louder as he swirls his tongue between his fingers, lapping up every drop of my blood and soothing the burn of my broken skin.

"Kryx," I wheeze, my arms falling away from his as air escapes my lungs and my vision blurs, the edges darkening.

"Stay with me, little vixen, or you won't get to take part in the fun," he says smoothly, his voice distant. The stinging of his claws on my throat subsides, and I breathe in deeply, my vision clearing with each inhale. I cough, forcing more air into my lungs as his fingers tangle in my hair, tugging hard at the roots. "Such a good girl," he croons, licking his lips. "But still, oh so naughty."

"Kryx," I snap, the burn in my lungs easing. "What the fuck?" He smirks as his mouth angles over mine, his sharp teeth scraping my bottom lip before sucking it into his mouth. He kisses me deeply, silencing any plea or cry as I press my hands against his chest, feeling the dense muscles flex beneath my fingers.

His free hand moves to my breast, palming it through my shirt before taking my budding nipple between his finger and thumb. He twists and pinches, forcing a scream from me that he swallows whole. He's worse than any monster I've ever let into my bed, but even as fear builds beneath my skin, threatening to tear through, I cling to him tighter, never wanting to let him go.

The room darkens, shadows swirling around us, snaking across my skin and binding my wrists and ankles, pressing me flat against the mattress. He pulls away with a sly smile, and I open my mouth to protest, but just as my lips part, a shadow slips over my mouth, gagging me as it coils around my head like a bridle.

Kryx towers over me, his massive body making me feel small. His nostrils flare as he inhales deeply through them. "Little vixen," he purrs, sounding like a lion stalking its prey. "Are you scared?" His eyes flash as the shadows tighten their grip on me, running a clawed finger across the shadowy straps that now press into my face, lifting the reins on his hooked finger. "You should be," he murmurs.

Sliding off the bed, he stands at the end, his eyes burning as brightly as the flames in the hearth. I try to speak, gnashing my teeth against the gag. I should be begging him to let me go—to stop this madness and leave me alone.

But that's not really what I want, is it?

I want the demon of Christmas to drag me to Hell and fuck me like the monster he is. I want him to claim me as his and keep me locked in this cabin for eternity. I want to be nothing more than his naughty human—to be used until he gets tired of me and discards me like a broken toy.

It's what I deserve.

The truth pushes against the bit of the shadow bridle, but I swallow it back down, where I crumple it into a ball and toss it into the fire, watching it burn into nothing but a lump of coal and turn to ash on my tongue.

I'll never admit to him that I *am* scared, but not in the way he thinks I am. I shouldn't feel this way about a demon—especially not one who has haunted my dreams for years, fucked with me, and hidden himself from existence. I should have run for the hills the first night he showed up here and gotten as far away as possible. It's not like I don't have the resources to go anywhere I want, easily change my identity, and live out the rest of my shitty life in hiding.

But instead, I stayed, because the truth is I'm tired of running.

It would almost be a relief for the ghosts of my past to finally catch up to me—maybe even run me over until I'm nothing more than a pile of roadkill. I've done what I needed to do to survive for so long that I've forgotten what it's like to truly live —to enjoy life. This is supposedly the most magical time of the year, but what they didn't say is that the magic is dark, burying you under heaps of snow until you're just an icy shell begging for some semblance of warmth.

What I didn't expect was for a demon to appear, with the power to not only thaw me, but burn me alive. His heat melts me, molding me like glass. My whole life is in his hands, where at any moment, he could let me fall and shatter into a million pieces.

A shadow slithers under my shirt and splits in two, each tendril curling around my nipples, gripping them tightly. Another shadow slips over my shirt, tearing it open. It falls away, exposing me, and I see the flames in Kryx's eyes intensify as he drags his gaze over my body, sprawled out before him. A slight tic tugs at his jaw as his muscles twitch, a predator ready to pounce. But he remains frozen, watching as his shadows taunt and tease me, pulling me closer to the edge.

Another one pushes past the waistband of my sleep pants, gently brushing against my inner thighs, the tip of it seeming to touch every incision left behind of his bite mark—almost tickling me. I groan around the bridle as another one wriggles past my lips and presses against the back of my throat, making me gag. "You're so fucking wet, Nicolette," Kryx growls, his eyes fixed on my center as if he has x-ray vision. His trembling hands curl into fists. "Fucking *soaked.*"

The shadow teases my entrance as another slides through my slit. My eyes roll back in my head as my body heats, and my desire drips and soaks into the fabric of my pants. But just as the embers spark into flames, the shadows pull back, leaving a chill that creeps over my skin.

I whimper as I lift my head, a look of desperation on my face, only to see Kryx completely cloaked in shadows, with only his flame-filled eyes visible. A ripping sound echoes from my lower body as a shadow slices through my pants, roughly yanking them off and tossing them on the floor.

I'm left completely exposed and restrained, my pussy dripping and my clit pulsing as the shadows retreat. I beg and plead in my mind, hoping the words will come out, but they're only stuck in my throat. I'm so fucking turned on that if he laid even one clawed finger on me, I would come right then.

"Is that all it would take, little vixen?" His rough voice swirls around me, almost as if he's inside my mind. *"One little touch?"*

Fuck. He *is* in there. Has he been able to read my mind this entire time? I push my thoughts, pressure building between my eyes, still desperately hoping he can hear me. *"Please, Kryx,"* I beg. *"Touch me. Fuck me."*

His shadows slowly creep up my body until they, once again,

find my nipples. Teasing me, the tendrils flick at the sensitive buds, causing my back to arch. They caress my skin, leaving goosebumps in their wake. The ones bound at my ankles release me, but my relief is short-lived as they force my knees to bend, wrapping around my legs and once again holding me in place. I'm more exposed in this position, giving Kryx an even better view of my pussy.

A low growl echoes through my head, vibrating down my body all the way to my aching clit. I take a deep breath through my nose as more shadows explore my body. One teases my ass while another slides through my slit, pressing against my entrance.

"Please," I cry out in my mind as he edges me even harder by swirling my clit a few times and pausing too long before beginning again. A tear slides down my face as I choke on the shadow that starts to fuck my mouth, its patience finally spent.

"I'm going to fill you up..." His voice vibrates through me again, straight to my core. *"And make you come again, and again, and again. And then, when your body gives out, I'll continue to fuck you in your dreams, tearing you to shreds until I tell you to wake up."*

More tears stream down my face as I gag, his shadow pressing even further down my throat, making me choke. The one at my ass roughly teases me just as it fills me. I cry out, but only a gagged sound escapes my lips, hot tears causing my vision to blur.

The other shadow pushes past the entrance of my pussy, thrusting in and out of me in sync with the one going in and out of my ass, making me feel entirely too full. They continue to play with my clit while pinching and pulling my tender nipples. I can't decide if I'm about to pass out or come to, but all I keep thinking about is wishing one of these shadows was Kryx—that it was his thick, throbbing, pierced cock pounding into my needy cunt.

"It will be soon, little vixen," he croons. *"If only you could see how*

fucking beautiful you are like this. Every hole filled to the brim with my shadows, and you at my mercy. It's the gift I've been patiently waiting for."

His words send me over the edge, and I come so hard that every muscle in my body tightens. The shadows in my throat, along with the one bridled on my face, fade away, finally allowing me to scream out. "Kryx," I gasp as I draw a mouthful of air into my lungs. "Oh, *God.*"

A hoof slams against the floor, rattling the entire cabin, and a clawed hand roughly grabs my face, but when I open my eyes, it's nothing more than a blur of shadows looking back at me. "Do *not* call to him," he bites out. This time, the words fill the room instead of my mind. *"I* am your god now. Your monster. Your *demon.* My name is the only one to leave your lips. *Mine."*

His invisible hand pulls away as his shadows pick back up where they left off, building me only to shatter me over and over until the room finally turns black, and I am lost in a sea of ecstasy-filled dreams, drowning in the waves of pleasure.

CHAPTER 12

Kryx

I stand at the edge of the thick forest, gazing out at her dreamscape, which has only grown darker over the years. It was once lush and green, with sunlight filtering through the canopy and the air filled with birdsong—a delicate place full of wonder and innocence.

But now? Only the light of a bright, full moon casts shadows on the cold, hard ground. That naivety and joy have faded, and she is now filled with sharp branches and thorns, catching and tearing open old, festering wounds.

To most, the change might seem alarming, but for me, it's perfection. Nicolette has been burned far too much in her life, and she bears the scorch marks as proof. Yet, just as I can easily walk through snow heaps, she can run through flames that lick her skin and emerge shining like blown glass.

I keep my hooves silent as I stalk through the forest, cloaking myself in shadows, and begin my hunt. Her scent surrounds me, but she's still far ahead as she races through the thickets, knowing the hidden shortcuts in her mind. Her heart beats in sync with mine, and her rapid breaths feel like she's breathing down my neck, even as she tries to run.

But she can never escape me.

"*I love the chase, little vixen,*" I say in my mind, letting it whisper into hers. "*But you know... no matter how far you try to run, I'll always catch you.*"

I'm met with only silence, but her scent of fear is carried in by the winds of the storm that clouds her mind. My rabid side is emerging, darkening my veins and sharpening my teeth. If it's the monster she wants, then it's the monster she'll get.

The trees move and bend out of my way, creating a clear path directly to her and making this far too easy. I step over the stream that cuts through this part of the forest, careful not to disturb the water that rushes through it, frost forming like crystals on the banks. Her pulse thrums through me, vibrating to my core as I pick up my pace.

Her scent is wildly intoxicating, filling the open air as I step through the tree line into a dark valley. I see movement below as Nicolette stumbles naked through the lush, knee-high grass. Fireflies drift around her, illuminating her fiery red hair—guiding her like a beacon in the night.

My lips curl into a fiendish grin, and I slow my pace even more, still hiding beneath my shadows, letting her believe she's made her escape. I can't help but give her a false sense of security, letting it wrap around her like a plush blanket, shielding her from the cold, cruel world.

She slows to a stop, looks around with bright, wild eyes, and leans against a large boulder, trying to catch her breath. I don't miss the pair of glowing orbs on the other side of the clearing, a horrific Nightmare waiting to devour her—one that doesn't stand a chance against me.

I am her sweetest dream and her darkest nightmare.

I am her shield and the knife at her throat.

I am her salvation and ruin.

And she is _mine_.

I watch as the Nightmare creeps closer, stepping into the

clearing and drawing nearer to her. It's more terrifying than any monster that could emerge from Hell. Its coal-black skin is stretched taut over its body as it constantly shifts into different creatures, changing even faster the closer it gets. It senses her fears, its long, gray tongue dripping with saliva as it licks its lips, nicking its rows of razor-sharp teeth. Dank, black blood begins to drip down its jaw.

I cast my shadows wide, keeping them close to the ground so as not to attract attention. These fucking Nightmares are clever, knowing exactly how and where to strike, and where there's one, there are usually many more. I need to be strategic in hunting it down before it tries to consume Nicolette, not letting her go until it has had its fill of her terror.

But what this Nightmare doesn't realize is that I'm far worse, and I'm the only monster allowed to sink its teeth into her and devour her, basking in the blood and carnage.

Nicolette Evergreen is mine to destroy, mine to fuck, and mine to protect—especially from herself.

My shadows slither like vipers, ready to bare their fangs and inject their poison into our enemy. They silently surround the Nightmare, one lifting itself just high enough to strike, wrapping around its maw like a muzzle to silence its screams as the others follow. They pile on and bring the Nightmare down in seconds, wrapping tightly like a boa constrictor, squeezing until it combusts into a cloud of inky black smoke.

The commotion draws Nicolette's attention, her head whipping around to glance over her shoulder, her body leaning against the boulder—perfect distraction for me to make my move. My cloak of shadows falls away as I step into the clearing, quickly closing the gap between us as I approach from behind her. She doesn't sense me coming until it's too late, my claws itching to sink into her skin and leave more of my marks, ones to remind the Nightmares that they are no longer the worst thing lurking in her mind.

Nicolette screams as I pull her to me, her back firmly against my chest. I clamp my hand over her mouth to silence her, pressing her ass against my hard cock. "Did you think you could escape me, little vixen?" I say into her ear, my breath clouding and tickling her skin. "Did you think that you could fall into your dreamscape and take respite in your naughty fantasies?" I tsk. "So naive."

I run my hand down her body, taking my time to explore her curves before I slide my finger between her folds—her cunt dripping. "You like the chase, do you?" I breathe in the scent of her hair, her curls cascading down her back and tickling my chest. "And you were so desperate to be caught. I can smell it." I flick my tongue out and lick up the shell of her ear. "Fucking *taste* it."

She melts into me, a moan slipping out between my fingers where I still cover her mouth. Her muscles twitch, resisting the pleasure; her instincts are urging her to run. I lower my hand, dragging my fingers over her full lips and scraping my claws down her throat, across her collarbone, and to her breast, rolling her nipple between my finger and thumb, giving her exactly what she wants.

Her hips buck as I swirl my finger around her clit, pressing her ass against me. "Kryx," she moans, her head falling back against my chest, her knees nearly buckling. "*Please.*"

The desperation in her voice as my name slips from her lips nearly makes me come. "Tell me what you want, Nicolette, and I just might give it to you," I say smoothly, listening to her quiet gasps as they fill the cold air like puffs of smoke. "What's at the top of your list?"

"*You,*" she breathes as she arches her back, pressing her breast further into my hand and grinding her ass into me. "I want *you.*"

"Oh, my little vixen, you already have me," I say before dragging my tongue down to her jaw. "Tell me what you want me to *do* to you."

"I want you to fuck me, Kryx," she says with a gasp, even as her voice becomes more commanding. "I want to feel your cock as you pound into me. *Claim* me. Make me *yours*."

My cock twitches with her every word, and I nearly come apart at the seams. I spin her around and force her onto her knees. "On your back with your knees up," I grit out as I fight the urge to just fuck her senseless. She lowers herself back onto the grass and takes her position. "Such a fucking good girl," I croon from where I still stand over her. "So good, yet so fucking *bad*."

I drop to my knees, lift her legs over my shoulders, and bring myself down to her pussy, where it glistens in the moonlight like the most precious gem. She watches me down her body as I tease her with my tongue, her thighs tightening around my head. She runs her fingers over one of my horns, curling them tightly around it. My body shivers at her touch, but I refuse to let her flip the script and tear me apart like a present on Christmas morning.

She moans as my shadows lower her back to the ground, pinning her hands above her head. "Let me touch you," she begs, but I know better than to let her continue—I'd be a fucking goner.

I flick and swirl my tongue, bringing her higher and higher, preparing to push her over the edge just as I did before she became lost in her dreams. Her thighs clamp around my head, keeping me in place as my name becomes a soft chant. I slide my hands under her ass and let my claws prick her skin. Her back arches and her breaths become erratic as she nears her release.

My aching cock presses against my pants, staining them with my precum as it begs for her pussy. She tastes so sweet on my tongue—like sugarplums—that it makes my teeth hurt. The near constant urge to bite into her soft, supple skin is almost overwhelming as her legs tighten and her hips buck against my mouth.

"*Fuck,*" she bites out, squirming in my hold. "I-I'm going to come."

My cock twitches with each panting moan she makes, my own release tingling at the base of my spine. "*Come for me, little vixen,*" I say into her mind. "*Scream my name and remind every monster here who you belong to. Tell them who is the only one who can hurt you and save you. The only one who can push you over the edge of insanity and catch you before you fall.*"

She shatters in my hands; her cum coats my tongue as she screams my name, shaking the ground beneath us while the edges of the clearing start to blur. A curtain of darkness falls over us, turning the inside of her mind black—tearing her away from me as she snaps awake.

CHAPTER 13

Nicolette

My eyes snap open as I take a deep, shuddering breath. The edges of my vision are blurry, but I would recognize my bedroom anywhere. Panic overtakes me as I pull my hand away from between my aching legs, my fingers glistening in the firelight as my cum drips from them, soaking the sheets.

"*Kryx*," I bark as I sit up, yanking the covers off my sweat-slicked body. I slide out of bed, pulling the sheet off with me and wrapping myself in it as I keep shouting his name, my panic turning into anger. "What the *fuck* was that? And where the *fuck* are you?"

I stomp into the living room, expecting him to be there with his fucking malicious smirk plastered on his face, but the room is empty, and the only sounds are the howling wind outside and the crackling fire. The flames that were burning in my chest are doused with ice-cold water.

He's not here.

Once again, I'm completely alone.

I back slowly into my bedroom, feeling the urge to shower— needing to wash away the sensation of him as it crawls across my skin. I need to silence the voice in my head that sounds just like him and come to my senses.

He's a monster—a demon.

And here I am, utterly devastated to wake up once again and find that he's not here—that he didn't stay. He keeps claiming that I'm his, but he doesn't get to own me if he's constantly abandoning me in my most vulnerable moments, like everyone else has. He's making me look weak, and I haven't fought for years to master the art of fucking people over—keeping everyone at arm's length—just to be fucked with by an imaginary beast from the North Pole.

"Fuck you," I say through gritted teeth into the empty room. "I'm *done* with you. I'm *done* with your games. Leave me alone and don't come back." I hope that wherever he is, he can fucking hear me.

I stumble into the bathroom and turn the shower to the hottest setting I can handle, letting the burn seep into my skin and turn me red. I scrub my skin with my loofah, desperately trying to remove any traces of him, watching as it all goes down the drain. The anger that was left suddenly shifts, and my tears mix with the water pouring over my head, burning my skin even more.

How could I be so fucking stupid to think that a monster—no different from me—would stick around after getting what it wanted? What was owed? That I would be anything more than a toy for him to play with until he grew bored and finally threw me away?

Breaking me.

I run my hands down my body, letting my fingers trace over my curves, and the dark little voice in my mind makes me question whether he finally saw me for who I am, and I repulsed him. Whatever rose-colored glasses were clouding his judgment were ripped away, and he came to his senses, just like everyone else, beating me at my own game.

I'm a con artist by trade. I don't need to be pretty to pretend to be someone else and take naive, cheating men for all they're worth. My ability to manipulate them and discard them is no different from what Kryx has done to me. We can both sniff out the shit, and that's all I am.

A piece of fucking shit.

I stay in the shower until the water runs cold, and even then, I stand there for a few more minutes, letting it freeze me to my core until my teeth begin to chatter.

I cut the water, and the steam continues to fill the bathroom, coating every surface with a glossy sheen. I dry off and wrap myself in my favorite robe. It's dark gray and reaches to my ankles, made of soft sherpa fabric, perfect for cold winter nights like this, but still unable to thaw my icy, frost-bitten heart.

I grip the sink and take a deep breath, trying to dislodge the lump in my throat and untie the knot in my chest. Using my sleeve, I wipe the steam from the glass and look at myself. My breath catches as I'm met with the reflection of those same fiery red eyes that have watched me for what feels like a lifetime. The ones that haunt my dreams but are so familiar they've started to feel like a home I don't necessarily want to escape from.

Kryx watches me through the mirror, his gaze burning hot. How dare he show up here again? I want to scream at him, tell him to get the hell out and never come back. But every cruel word gets caught in my throat as I stare back at his reflection, not sure if he's really behind me or if it's all still a fucking dream.

A living nightmare.

"Little vixen." His voice is a deep timbre that washes over me, gently caressing my skin. "Is that what you really believe?"

I cringe at the pity in his voice and the soft look in his eyes. I grip the sink tighter and squeeze my eyes shut, refusing to let him see the tears gathering behind them.

"Do you think I cannot hear your thoughts? That I can't feel the ache in your chest as if it's my own?" He shifts on his feet, his hoof clicking on the tile floor as he steps further into the small bathroom, towering over me.

His clawed finger brushes against my neck, and his scent of embers and pine fills my nostrils, awakening every cell in my body. My knees threaten to buckle, and my arms tremble as I try to hold myself up. The steam makes it hard to breathe, and hot tears brim at the corners of my eyes.

He's the one who ripped open my never-healing wound with his nightmare, dragging me back into my childhood home and forcing me to relive the parts of my life I've locked away. And even though I blame him for the searing-hot pain that pulses through me, I want him to be the one to wrap it in bandages.

To fix it.

To finally heal me.

But I refuse to let him in—to see the broken pieces that threaten to gut me and let him see me bleed out. Because every person I've ever let into my life has left me high and dry, making it clear that I'm an unlovable monster—a nightmare myself.

His knuckles brush across my jaw, and instead of succumbing to the rush his touch triggers, my eyes flash open, and I spin around to face him, letting the anger that ignites in my veins explode. "Fuck you," I snap, the harsh words ringing out, bouncing off the tiles.

I reach up and slap his cheek, causing his head to whip to the side from the impact, his long black hair curtaining his face. "How dare you come back here? How dare you continue to string me along as if I'm nothing but a child's toy? A toy for you to use. To fucking break." I suck in a breath as the fire inside me rages on. "Get. The fuck. *Out.*"

I press my finger into his chest and then point to the door behind him, signaling for him to leave. His eyes blaze bright as he stares down at me, a look of shock on his face. He calls me his, but I don't belong to anyone. And I never will.

"Why would I ever leave you, Nicolette?" he asks, his voice turning into a low growl.

My mouth gapes, and my cheeks burn with anger. "Because you have come into my home, into my dreams, into my *life*, and have left me time and time again." I step back, pressing myself against the edge of the sink, trying to create more space between us. "You love to see me begging. You love the pain that you cause. But what do I get out of this? I'm fucking done with your games, and I want you to leave me alone."

He closes the gap, placing his large hands on either side of me, trapping me in. I size him up. His broad, muscular chest rises and falls as if he's barely holding on. His long black hair cascades around his chiseled jaw and broad shoulders. His onyx-black horns curl backward, absorbing all the light in the room as his shadows grow wider behind him.

My eyes lift, and I meet his gaze. His crimson eyes are breathtakingly terrifying as the irises flicker like flames, warming the cold, dark corners of my soul even as my own fire rages and spreads through me.

"I have *never* left you," he breathes as the words swirl around him like smoke. "And I never intend to."

My hands curl into fists, nails sharply digging into my palms. "Then explain the empty room, and now the empty bed. I've only ever woken up alone with cold, bitter sheets next to me and an empty feeling in my chest."

This little dance we've been doing has finally gone too far, since he's seen too much of me. I'm walking a dangerous line I can't cross, and neither can he. He was here to punish me, and he more than succeeded; he's completely shattered me. I feel a sob rising in my throat, but I push it back down. I refuse to let him see how broken I am from the way he fumbled and dropped me, fragmenting me into a million pieces, with no one here to help me pick them up, and leaving me with bloody fingertips.

He infiltrated my dreams for years, erasing any memory of them as if he had permission to do so, but he couldn't hide the truth about my shitty life. The same shitty life I gave up on. I moved out, moved away, and moved on when I realized I couldn't fix something that was shattered and broken, just like I can't fix myself.

His eyes flicker like flames as he stiffens, claws digging into the porcelain sink while my words linger heavy between us. "I couldn't leave you even if I wanted to, Nicolette." His deep voice softens.

"But I want you to," I bite. "I *need* you to."

He looks down at me, the fire in his eyes flickering to glowing embers. "I can't," he says softly, an edge of pain in his voice.

I press my hands into his chest, feeling his thundering heart beneath my palm as I try to push him away, but he doesn't move. "Why? Why can't you just leave me alone? I know I'm a piece of shit who needs to be punished, but I'm nowhere close to being like some of the worst people in the world. Those are the ones you need to go after, not me. Yes, I'm a fucking criminal, but all I want is to be left alone to suffer in solitude."

"The first time I saw you," he starts, his muscles rippling beneath my palms as he takes a shallow breath. "I felt something deep inside me that I tried to ignore but couldn't. I've thought about you every fucking day since. And then you showed up on my list, and I took the opportunity to use your punishment for my own gain."

I watch him as his words sink in, a strange feeling building in my chest. "What?" I snap, pushing him away, and this time, he steps back. "What are you fucking talking about? *What* first time?"

He averts his eyes for a moment, seeming to collect his thoughts before looking back at me. "The first time I saw you, nearly twelve years ago, in your childhood home... with your mother."

My heart races, pumping blood through my body at lightning speed, flushing my cheeks. "Why would my mother be on your list? She's never done anything wrong in her life. And she's fucking *ill*." I avert my gaze as he stands motionless before me, his hands clenched at his sides.

I think back to all the nights she slept on the couch in front of the Christmas tree, the one she refused to take down, as if she were waiting for Santa to slide down the chimney and bring back her joy. I watched for years as she started to change, seeming to wither away.

Breaking.

My eyes snap up to his, another surge of fury flooding through me. "Were you the one she was always waiting on?" I choke out. "The reason for her misery?"

His brows are knit together when I finally look back at him. "I visited your mother... often," he admits. "However, I can assure you that I was not someone she was waiting to see." He visibly leans forward as if his body is being pulled toward mine. "And if I could have helped it, I would have never come to see her again."

"Then who was she waiting for?" I snap, taking a step toward him. "If it wasn't you, then who the fuck was it?"

He shakes his head, his long black strands catching on the harness strapped across his chest. I reach out and grip the warm leather, jerking him toward me. I stare into his eyes, searching for answers—for his lies.

"My mother is a good person," I growl. "So, tell me, Krampus, why was she on your list so often? What did she do that was so terrible that she was forced to endure your torture? Was it because she birthed a monster like me? Married one like my father?"

He looks down at where my hand is, the veins in his forearms darkening as he clenches his fists tighter at his sides, but his face remains solemn. "I'm not always told the crimes of my victims," he says lowly. "I am instructed by the list on how harsh to make the punishments, and I'm inclined to listen."

"And how harsh was hers?" I ask, my hand trembling as I grip the harness tightly. He stands silently, his body stiffening as he breaks our gaze. "Tell me," I say desperately, shaking him. "Don't fucking lie to me, Kryx."

His eyes flick back to mine as his shoulders slump. "*Torturous*," he whispers, pain clear in his voice.

I let my hand fall away, the sound of my heart cracking audible in my ears. "You... you broke her," I say, a sob working its way up my throat. "*You* did this to her."

"There's a reason she was on my list, Nicolette," he says flatly, replacing the pain that was once so evident in his voice. "Whether you are to believe her a good person or not—"

"Your list was *wrong*," I shout, and a sob finally escapes me. "You were fucking *wrong*."

He steps closer, grabbing my shoulders as I try to push him away, hot tears streaming down my face. "The list is never wrong," he says softly. "I'm sorry, little vixen. I am."

"How could you?" My words catch as a sob, the fight slowly leaving my body, turning my anger into sorrow.

He pulls me close and wraps his arms around me, leaving me no choice but to lean into him. "I'm magically bound to that list, Nicolette, and I fought to defy its orders when I saw your mother becoming ill and her mind slowly slipping away. However, I have no choice but to cross her name off, or the magic will eventually force me to do so. After I finished, I took her memories and as much of her pain as I could, similar to what I did with you. She woke up knowing she had had a nightmare, but she didn't remember anything about it. I tried to stay away for as long as I could, but eventually, the list left me no choice but to follow its commands."

I curl my arms around his torso, resting my hands on his back and curling my nails into his skin, tearing it open and anchoring me to him. The cracks in my heart continue to grow with every breath, splintering the edges and making it even more jaded.

"Who comes up with the list?" I ask from where my face is pressed to his chest. "Maybe they can explain what her crime was."

He glides his hand up my back, gently lacing his fingers through my hair, while his other arm stays firmly wrapped around my waist. "It's not a person, but dark, ancient magic that creates the list. It goes far beyond any power Nick and I have. It was put in place so we would remain equals and could not influence the other to put someone on our lists." His chest vibrates with every word, my body thrumming as if in reply.

I tilt my head back and look up at him, his gentle gaze meeting mine. "Is my name still on the list?" I ask, his fingers tightening in my hair.

"Not anymore," he says quietly. "The punishments I've doled out have more than sufficed." I catch a ghost of a smile on his lips, a twitch happening in the corner of mine.

"Then why are you still here, Kryx?" I ask. Even in my soft tone, the question sounds harsh, but I don't mean it that way. If he's bound by magic, then he should have moved on by now.

"Like I said, I couldn't leave even if I wanted to, not since..." He trails off as the wind outside picks up, smashing against the side of the house. I stay silent while he searches for the words.

He takes a deep breath, his eyes meeting mine as warmth fills my chest. "I've felt this unending pull toward you ever since I first saw you, Nicolette. I tried to ignore it, but the feeling only intensified. It wrapped around my neck like a noose and pulled me toward wherever you were."

He pulls his hand out of my hair and hooks a finger under my chin, tilting my head back even further. "It wasn't until I stood outside this cabin that my control snapped—the need to have you overtook me, and all the jagged pieces fell into place." He slides his hand up, cupping my face as if it's something so precious that he risks it crumbling in his hand.

"What pieces?" I ask, my brows stitching together. "What are you talking about?"

His mouth opens and closes like a fish out of water, seeming to suffocate on his words. His body tenses as he squeezes his eyes shut, with a deep crease forming between his brows. "Why do you think that I can hear your thoughts, Nicolette?" he asks, the words flickering brightly like the fire crackling in the living room, a gust of wind blowing through the dampener.

"Because you're a demon and demons can read minds," I reply as a chill runs up my spine, his shadows curling around us like featherless wings.

He snorts, nostrils flaring. "While it's true that I'm a demon, I cannot hear everyone's thoughts, little vixen. Only *yours*."

"Why only mine? Is there something wrong with me?" I ask as his hand slides to my throat, running his finger across my jaw.

"No. There's nothing wrong with you, little vixen," he says with a chuckle that eases some of the tension. "The reason I can hear your thoughts and feel your most profound emotions is because you are my—"

His words are drowned out by the wild wind outside, along with a sharp knock at the door. We both turn and step out of the bathroom, Kryx positioning himself in front of me as a blast of frost-bitten air blows past us, extinguishing the fire and plunging us into darkness.

CHAPTER 14

Kryx

I stand firm between Nicolette and the door, watching as it rattles on its hinges, the bitter cold seeping through the cracks. The air shifts as I try to light the fire, snuffing out every attempt. While there are plenty of people who would seek revenge for Nicolette's crimes, no mortal is out there. No one would be foolish enough to come this far out in a blizzard like this, and we are deep into the night, hours from dawn, giving the monsters a chance to emerge.

I take a step toward the door, but she grips my arm. "Kryx," she whispers, fear tinging my name. "*Wait.*"

I glance at her over my shoulder, pressing my finger to my lips, hoping she can see me through the dark and step away. I sneak through the cabin, careful to keep my hooves quiet as I approach the door. I catch a glimpse of someone outside and lean closer for a better look, the glass covered in a thick frost.

Fuck.

I look back at Nicolette, motioning for her to hide as her eyes widen. She turns and rushes into her bedroom, leaving the door wide open. I open my mouth to protest, but hear the soft click of her closet door as she shuts herself inside.

Taking a deep breath, I curl my fingers around the door handle, the cold immediately seeping into my skin, causing steam to rise from between my fingers. I yank open the door and wrap my clawed hands around the neck of the man on the other side, throwing him into the snow. I launch myself out the door, landing on the ice with a loud crunch.

My fiery rage pulses through me, heating me and causing the snowflakes to sizzle on my skin as I look down at the last motherfucker I would ever allow near Nicolette.

Jack fucking Frost.

"Hello, Krampus," he says slyly, voice edged with menace, as I tighten my grip on his throat.

I straddle him and lean forward, meeting his gaze and baring my teeth. "What the *fuck* are you doing here, Jack?"

He grins a Cheshire smile, his blue-tinted lips stretching ear to ear. "Nick wanted me to see where you've been disappearing to lately, and I'm not going to lie, I'm pretty fucking curious myself."

I tighten my grip on his throat, allowing my claws to sink into his snow-pale skin until his once-crimson blood bleeds as blue as an icy sea. "I don't believe for a second that Nick sent you. What do you fucking want, Jack?"

He lies in the snow as the arctic wind howls around us, assaulting my exposed skin that even my hellfire blood can't entirely fend off. It curls around my arms, trying to pull me away from him. He traded his soul to become Nick's malevolent guardian, wielding ice and snow as his weapons, but he will never be stronger than me. I was born a demon, with the darkness of Hell ingrained in every cell of my being. His command over winter weather is strong, but he has no chance against me.

I summon my own power, shadows curling around him like a cocoon as I pull my hand away, slicing his skin. His smile falters, and his eyes go wide as they lock him in tight, cutting off his magic and forcing him into a deep sleep. The blizzard winds around us roar, the storm a monster of its own, as my shadows tighten their hold like a vise, keeping him exactly where I want him.

As my eyes flutter shut, I step into his dreamscape. The icy tundra he has created in his mind is a vast white landscape, scattered with a few holly bushes, and a distant forest of snow-capped evergreens swaying in the wind. I turn to see Jack sitting on a throne of glassy ice in the middle of the valley, with streams of frigid-blue water winding around it.

He watches me, his pale blue eyes darkening as I approach. "You're a fucking coward," he growls. "You can't even face me in the real world? You have to force yourself into my dreams to do what? Teach me a lesson?" Branches snap around him, Nightmares lurking in the woodland that surrounds us, waiting for the right moment to overtake him and drown him in his own fears.

"Nick would never send you to check on me, so tell me, *Jack*, why the fuck are you here?" I growl. His eyes widen slightly as my shadows rise behind me in a silhouette of wings, flapping wide and sending a swirl of snow and wind around him.

He shifts in his throne, swinging his legs over the armrest as he lets out an exasperated breath. "Because, *Krampus*, you've been spending way too long in this neck of the woods." He chuckles at his failed attempt at a joke. "And I intend to see what has taken your attention away from the work you seem to love so much. Is it a *pet*, perhaps?"

My shadows curl past me and strike, yanking him up into a sitting position and binding him to the chair. My whips crack through the air as they appear in my hands, ready to deliver a well-deserved lashing as I take a step toward him. But instead of cowering in fear, he looks at me with a heated gaze, as if this is playing out like a dark fantasy.

"I could smell their desire from a mile away and watch it rise like steam through the cracks of the cabin. If you're trying to be discreet, you're doing a terrible job. What would Nick think if he knew you were playing with a broken toy? One that he would love to bring back to his workshop?" His tone is cold and cruel, and I can see the cogs in his mind turning as he attempts to outsmart me.

My rage pulses, shaking the ground and sending a crack through his throne. Shadows pull him from his seat and bring him to his knees at my feet. Chains replace them as they turn him away, anchoring him to the ground. He looks over his shoulder, his eyes filled with rage, baring his teeth. I flick my wrist, and my whips crack against his icy skin, shredding it. His screams echo through the valley, shaking the snow from the pines around us. The Nightmares back away, retreating into the darkness as they realize who the real monster is tonight.

His blue blood drips down his body and pools beneath my hooves, crystallizing in the snow. I reach down and grip his hair, yanking his head back and forcing him to look up at me. "You're going to stay out of my business and *far* the fuck away from anyone on *my* list. You've crossed the line, and next time, I won't be so fucking *nice*."

"I'll fucking tell Nick," he growls as he takes in sharp breaths through his nose, pain swirling in his eyes. "I'll tell him all about your little toy, and he'll make sure to take them for himself. And you know he *loves* to break things."

Leaning down, I snap my teeth in his face, causing him to flinch. *Pathetic.* "You seem to forget who's a demon and who isn't," I say coolly, my breath clouding between us. "And the only reason you're still breathing is because you let Nick sink his dick into you, and I'm not about to take that pleasure away from my oldest friend."

I lean closer and lower my voice further. "But if I find out you were anywhere near this cabin again, I will find you and break you. Then, I'll find someone shiny and new for Nick, and you will be forgotten—nothing more than a cheap throwaway. A stocking stuffer."

I release his hair, and he slumps forward into the snow, groaning in pain. "This isn't over, *Krampus*," he spits without even bothering to look back at me as he slowly crawls toward his throne. "You'd better watch out."

I step back and watch as he loses consciousness, falling face-first. I turn around, catching a glimpse of the lone Nightmare staring back at me from the tree line, waiting patiently for me to leave. I give it a nod as I tear open a door and step out of Jack's mind, leaving the Nightmare to its feast.

The warmth of the fire seeps into my skin as I step back into the cabin, the only sound the clicking of my hooves against the hardwood. "Nicolette?" I call out her name, but she doesn't answer. Panic rises in my veins, and I send out my shadows, having them search every corner of her home. Jack is a trickster, and he could have easily used himself as a distraction for something else to come in and take her, stealing what's *mine*.

I burst into her bedroom, the door flying open and the handle nearly lodging itself as it bangs against the wall. I flip the light switch, and a lamp in the corner turns on as the fire in the wood burner crackles. Everything seems in its place, with the closet door still closed.

I grip the knob, turning it slowly, then pull open the door, the hinges quietly squeaking. It's dark, the rod filled with clothes for every season. I crouch down carefully and catch sight of a pair of long legs, shifting and pulling in closer to the body attached.

The panic in my chest fades, replaced with a flicker of amusement as I part the clothes, revealing Nicolette. Her eyes are wide as she examines me, terror still lingering on her face. "Kryx," she breathes, her muscles easing.

"Little vixen, why are you still hiding? I called for you," I say softly, holding out my hand, but she doesn't reach for it; instead, she pulls her robe tighter around herself.

"I thought it might be a trap," she whispers, her gaze shifting past my head as if she's expecting someone else to be there. *For Jack.* "Who was that at the door? What happened?"

I growl as her fear floods my senses, weighing heavily on my skin. I should have slayed the bastard when I had the chance. But then I'd have to explain to Nick why I slaughtered his little spy, and I'm not sure how he would respond. Plus, it could put Nicolette in even greater danger, and I'm not willing to risk her over a pathetic guardian.

"Come out and I'll tell you," I say, offering her a gentle smile that seems to calm her. "There's no need to stay hidden now." This time, she reaches for my hand, slipping her fingers across my palm, sending a jolt of electricity up my arm.

I pull her to her feet, and just as if on cue, her robe falls open. She inhales sharply in surprise as her eyes flicker downward, but she remains still. I let my ravenous gaze wander over her, taking in her gorgeous breasts and alluring curves that lead right to her core, my bite a striking red tattoo on her otherwise smooth skin. The energy in the room shifts, her fear replaced by an almost palpable hunger.

"Oops," she whispers as her fingers trail over her breast, circling her nipple—*teasing me.* My cock twitches at her heated gaze as adrenaline continues to pump through my veins, her hand trailing down to her ribs and hips before coming around to her ass. She arches her back, letting her head fall back as she rakes her nails up her side and back to her breast, palming it.

What a naughty girl.

"Nicolette," I say lowly, her name a rumble in my chest— trying to claw its way out. "What are you doing?"

She drops her hand, and her robe slides from her shoulders, pooling at her feet. She remains silent as she turns, bending over to reveal her full ass and pussy, the latter glistening in the dim light. She delicately lifts her robe back up and looks at me over her shoulder, her green eyes twinkling.

I growl, holding myself back as she slides the robe back on, tying it tightly around her waist. She brushes past me toward the doorway, my fingers grazing her arm, but she quickly pulls away. Turning toward me, she holds up a hand, her eyes narrowing.

"No more touching. Not until you tell me everything," she says sharply, her commanding tone making me hard. She turns back and crosses into the living room.

Like a dog on a leash, I follow her, licking my lips. This woman is infuriating, teasing me like that and expecting me to be able to form a fucking sentence. "Nicolette," I warn as she lowers herself onto the couch, widening her legs and exposing her needy little cunt to me again.

"Tell me *everything*, Kryx," she says as she reaches down and cups her center, gliding her fingers through her folds. "And if I'm satisfied, then you can touch me—fuck me—all you want."

My mouth waters at the sight of her, my feral side threatening to pounce, and I hold back the groan that's rising in my throat. "I can't talk to you when you're sitting like that," I choke out, my jaw tense as fingers curl at my side.

She chuckles, her voice smooth as honey but dripping with poison. "I con men out of their money for a living, Kryx. That means I have to do whatever it takes to get what I want, and right now, this is the only way to make sure you tell me everything."

This woman has me by the fucking balls. No wonder she's at the top of the Naughty List.

She moves her fingers up and down, gliding in and out of

her slit. "I'm waiting," she says lowly as she continues to touch herself, her middle finger circling her entrance.

Fuck me.

"You're *never* getting off my Naughty List, little vixen," I growl, palming my hardened cock through my pants. "Fuck, Nicolette." I scrub my other hand over my face, my claw hooking on my bottom lip. "Do you know what you fucking do to me?"

The corners of her mouth tilt up, giving me a sly smile that disappears as quickly as it appeared. "Tell me why you've been infiltrating my dreams and stealing any memory of it, *Krampus.*" She bites out the last word, showing her teeth, pressing her finger into her cunt, and pumping it in and out.

She's an absolute fucking menace, her anger rising in the air and blending with the scent of her desire, crackling like embers. I stand and watch her, my mind flailing as I fight against my feral demonic side, which is waiting to finally claim her. She relaxes back, opening her robe to reveal her breasts. Her perfect, pink nipples harden at her touch, making my mouth water.

Her gaze narrows on me. "Since you claim not to know what you were punishing my mother for, let me ask this: how many times have you been sent to see her?"

I grip my cock, letting the pain clear my foggy mind. "I've been sent there for decades," I say with a growl, my throat tightening. "I was initially sent to punish your father, who became well acquainted with my whips and chains."

The energy in the room shifts as she gradually slows her touch, lifting her fingers and letting them hover over her center. She watches me, but her expression reveals nothing; her only tell is the slight flush of her cheeks.

"I assume you learned your profession from him?" I ask, and she gives me a curt nod, but her face remains neutral, her mind going silent.

"He was a piece of shit," she snaps, sitting up straight. "When

I was a teenager, he left us high and dry to run off with his assistant—who he'd been having an affair with for years—and start a whole new life with a brand-new family."

The wind outside howls, making the fire flicker and illuminating her green eyes with ire. "I had to figure out how to make money, to keep the roof over our heads, even as my mother worked herself to the bone. So, I used everything he taught me, and I beat him at his own game. Drained him fucking dry right before the Feds dragged him to the slammer and gave my mother every penny that bastard owed her."

I shift on my feet, inching toward her. "And he paid handsomely for his crimes," I say, trying to calm her anger and offer some reassurance. "In fact, I can make a special trip to his cell as my personal gift to you, and make sure he hasn't become too comfortable."

She averts her gaze, watching the flames that dance wildly, beckoning to her. "My mother is a *good* person, Kryx," she says softly, her brows furrowing. "If she did anything wrong in her life, it was staying with my father for as long as she fucking did. Your list must be wrong."

Shaking my head, I walk over to the couch and tower above her. "It's never been wrong, Nicolette. I can see you love your mother, but not everyone is who they seem. She was at the top of the list for a reason."

A small voice in the back of my mind fills my ears, buzzing like a mosquito. What if it was wrong? Magic has a mind of its own; it gives and takes, creating a balance in the world. However, Evelyn Evergreen was breaking, her mind crumbling. She wasn't aware of any crimes, nor did she give me the same feeling that most on the Naughty List do. I can sense it when someone is terrible, taste it like rot on my tongue, but hers tasted sour, like regret.

She shakes her head, clenching the fabric of her robe and covering herself, her cheeks flushing even more with anger. I can feel it in my chest as the flame intensifies and brightens. "Why was she on the list, Kryx? And don't lie to me."

"I don't know," I say roughly, my throat burning.

She jumps to her feet, her hands hitting my chest as she pushes me away. I'm caught off guard, taking a stiff step back, my hoof echoing through the room. "You're fucking lying," she shouts. "I'm a liar by trade, and I can sniff one out a mile away."

I stare down at her, her eyes turning glassy as tears gather in the corners. I clear my throat, the pain tearing through it, until I finally give in. "She had an affair first, Nicolette," I say, and even as the pain in my throat subsides with the truth spilling from my lips. A knot forms in my chest, making it hard to breathe. "It had been going on for a long time, and she—"

Nicolette moves and shoves me again, but this time, I don't budge. "You're a *liar*," she snarls. "That's what demons do, they fucking lie." She pounds her fists against my chest as a rogue tear falls, splashing onto me.

I hold her wrists, securing them as she lets out a furious scream, a sob escaping her lips. I pull her close to me, her forehead resting against my chest, tears sliding down her face and wetting my skin. I wrap my arms around her, holding her tightly. "I would never lie to you, Nicolette," I say calmly, refusing to feed off her wave of emotions even as my chest feels as if it's caving in. "I would never lie to my mate."

She stiffens, her head snapping back and her eyes widening as she gazes up at me. "What did you just fucking say?"

I hold her chin in my hand, gently pressing my claws into her jaw. "I said, I would never lie to my *mate*." I tilt her chin higher. "You are my mate, Nicolette." She looks back at me, her expression growing more panicked with each second that ticks by. "Why do you think we can speak to each other in our minds? That I can feel your emotions as if they are mine, tearing me apart and burning through my chest? You are *undeniably* my mate."

Her fingers wrap around my wrist, pressing into my pulse point and feeling my thundering heartbeats. She remains silent as the words continue to fall from my lips. "I tried to stay away, Nicolette. I tried to let you live a normal life, but when it became too much, I had to sneak into your dreams. It's why I stole them so that you would be none the wiser."

"But, Kryx, how—" she starts, but I press my thumb to her lips, silencing her words.

"But when your name showed up on the Naughty List, Nicolette, it was a sign. My chance to come crashing back into your life—to ruin it and ruin you." I lower my face, brushing my lips across hers. "To make you *mine*."

She sucks in a shuddering breath as her trembling hand comes up and cups my face. "Is that why you gave me those memories back? Not to scare me, but to let me see the truth?"

I press my cheek into her palm, feeling the electricity in her touch flutter through me. "Once we came face to face again, I couldn't hold on to them any longer, and they were not mine to keep. You deserved to see that we were meant to be together, no matter how painful it could be."

She averts her gaze, her lips parting. "I'm your *mate?*" she whispers, saying the word as if she's tasting a delicacy, rolling it across her tongue. "But... how is that even possible?"

"Fate," I say simply. In truth, it's the only answer I can think of, since no one knows how mates are chosen. I believe it was written in the cosmos, taking thousands of years to come to fruition, forcing me to search every corner of the world to fill the empty space in my chest. To make me whole. "And no one defies fate, little vixen. Not even a demon."

CHAPTER 15

Nicolette

The demon of Christmas is my mate.

My chest warms, and my body thrums as I look up at him. I feel like I should be concerned that a monster from a children's fairytale—a demon, for that matter—is my mate. This might explain why my relationships were always complete disasters and why I never felt anything for them. I'm shit at choosing men, so an actual demon being my mate makes a lot of sense.

"But... I'm *human*," I sputter, my mind caught in a whirlwind.

"I am not one to question fate," he says, running the back of his claws across my cheek. "And neither should you, little vixen, because not everything they give is considered a gift."

Cocking my head to the side, I take him in; he's so terrifyingly handsome that it makes me weak every time I look at him. He consumed my dreams and fought off my Nightmares, with flames in his eyes blazing as he watches me, warming me from the inside out.

"Why did you keep this from me all this time?" I ask. "Why didn't you tell me sooner?"

He presses his face into my hair, taking a deep breath

through his nose. "I wanted to give you the chance to live your life—to find someone who would make you happy and that wasn't, well... me. *Krampus*." His voice sounds almost sad as his words tangle into my mess of curls. "As badly as I craved you, I treated you like forbidden fruit, but you only kept ripening for me." He leans further down, his mouth just above mine, his tongue flicking out. "And you taste just as delicious in this realm as you do in your dreamscape—maybe even sweeter."

My cheeks keep heating up, spreading down my neck and straight to my core, swirling wildly. "Does this happen a lot with demons? Human mates?"

He shrugs, bringing his mouth even closer to mine, our breaths mingling. "I don't regularly converse with many of the other demons who reside in this realm besides Nick, and I certainly don't share the details of my proclaimed mate with them, especially since I haven't claimed you yet."

I pull back and look up at him, frowning. "Wait. There are other demons? How do they get here? Have they been summoned, like with an Ouija board or dark magic?"

He laughs, the sound like a storm, swirling around me. "Little vixen, there are many beings that reside in this realm and feast upon it. The veil between worlds is far thinner than you can imagine. However, I was sent by the devil himself, not summoned by a mere human looking for a thrill. Don't believe everything you hear."

My cheeks flush with embarrassment as I let out a scoffed laugh. Yes, this giant monster in front of me is a creation of Hell, but is Hell truly the desolate place it was portrayed to be by men hiding behind their sins? Or is it actually a place of salvation where people like my parents, or eventually me, go to spend their afterlife?

"I'll show you someday," he says softly, brushing his lips against mine, the taste of him seeping into my mouth.

"How does this work? You and me?" The question slips from my lips as he pulls away. "Do I become a demon, too?"

He chuckles again, his eyes sparkling with joy. "You will not become a demon, but once you accept me as your mate, your soul will become bound to mine and you will live an immortal life... with me." He pauses, as if he's waiting for me to run the other way. "But only if this is what you want."

The warmth in my chest spreads as I take him in, from his striking horns and hellfire eyes to his colossal hooves. This is insane, right? Not only because I'm in the presence of one of the most infamous demons, but also because I'm mated to him.

He punishes people, invading their dreams and becoming their worst nightmare. He could crush anyone just by flexing his hand, dragging them to Hell if he so desired. He's a monster in every sense of the word... to everyone but me.

In the past few days, this very demon has given me an escape and shown me pleasure beyond my wildest dreams. And is it so wrong to want to be a monster with him? To give him everything he's given me in return?

I look at him, and his eyes have fluttered closed, as if granting me my privacy. I slide my hands over his chest, pressing my palm against his thunderous heart until mine beats in sync. "Kryx," I say his name like a prayer, drawing his attention back to me as his eyes flash open.

"Nicolette." He says my name like a plea, as if he were dropping to his knees.

"I have known you for years of my life, and you have brought me the deepest pain and the greatest pleasure. I have craved you from the moment you walked into this cabin, my memories of you proving that my connection to you is real and not just another dream. My life has been nothing but betrayal and pain, one I've had to fight my way through, hoping I would come out on the other side." I sniff, tears collecting in my eyes as the truth pours from my lips.

As I delve deeper into the memories he returned to me, I realize he did more than just tie me up and fuck me; he protected me from the beasts lurking in the shadows of my mind, from the monstrous thoughts threatening to extinguish the fire within me. He did what was necessary, only the minimum required to satisfy the list. I close my eyes tight, and tucked away in the corner of my mind, I see Kryx curling up with me on the fur rug, running his hand through my hair, watching over me as I drift to sleep.

My heart feels trapped in a vise as tears sting behind my eyes, emotion threatening to overwhelm me. "Take my heart and my soul, Kryx. Make me yours in this life and the next."

He softly holds my face with his massive hands, his thumb wiping away a stray tear as it slips down my cheek. "You are the other half of me, little vixen," he breathes. "You will never face another day of suffering or real pain, only the immense pleasures I plan to inflict on you every day from now until the end of time."

He lowers his mouth, pulling me in for a deep, head-spinning kiss. His wicked, forked tongue tangles with mine as he steals the breath from my lungs. Heat pools between my legs as my body warms, his hands sliding down my back and gripping my ass, hoisting me up to him. I wrap my legs around his waist as he carries me to my room.

Not breaking the kiss, he gently lowers me onto the bed, his claws pricking me, sending a thrill up my spine. "Kryx," I moan into his mouth, letting him taste his name on my tongue. "*Claim me.*"

He pulls back, his eyes brighter than I've ever seen them. "I'm going to make you come on my face, and then I intend to take you slow and deep, little vixen," he growls, his voice rough. "And then I'm going to make you scream, letting everyone between the North Pole and Hell know who you belong to—who your *mate* is."

Heat curls in my abdomen so hot that my desire drips between my legs. He loosens the belt of my robe, baring my body to him as he licks his lips, his tongue flicking his snake bite piercings and leaving saliva in the corner of his mouth.

Swirling his tongue over the tip of my nipple, he has me arching my back and letting out a quiet moan. He scrapes his teeth across the sensitive skin of my breast before licking away the pain. His large hand circles my throat, guiding my head back against the mattress. He nips, sucks, and licks across my skin, touching every part of me as if he's never tasted me before, leaving his mark on every inch.

The cool caress of his shadows tickles my skin as they brush against me, waiting for his command as he slides down and rests his head between my legs. His long tongue flicks out, lashing at my already throbbing clit. The sudden contact causes me to gasp and arch my back as he guides my legs over his shoulders, gripping my ass and lifting my hips. "As sweet as winterberry wine," he says as he glides his tongue between my folds, teasing my entrance. "A feast waiting to be devoured."

His tongue plunges into me, curling and hitting my G-spot, the prick of his claws sending me higher. "Kryx," I pant as I reach down and grip his horns, trying to hold on as he continues to drive me closer to the edge.

He groans, the sound vibrating through my core. "I love how my name sounds on your tongue as your desire coats mine."

One of his shadows brushes against my ass, pressing into me, filling me. I moan at the quick slice of pain as it takes me, causing me to grind my hips into Kryx's face. The shadow remains still as I thrust my hips, doing all the work for it.

Kryx drags his teeth over my clit, filling my vision with the brightest stars. I scream his name as I fall into the abyss, squeezing my eyes shut as my orgasm overtakes me, drowning me in pleasure and making me gasp for air.

He slides my legs off his shoulders as he rises to his feet, unfastening his pants and letting them fall to the floor, releasing his monstrous cock. He stands there, sliding his hand up and down his length, the dark tip dripping precum, growing more erect with each stroke. The firelight reflects off his piercings that ascend his shaft. I rest on my elbows and admire his magnificent form, one that could easily be mistaken for a malignant god's.

I let my gaze drift over him, moving from his sharp, tense jaw to his broad chest and chiseled abs, down to his defined V that guides my hungry eyes to his engorged cock, each muscle flexing as he shifts on his hooves. The electricity in the air crackles between us, surging through my body. "You're glorious," I say, my imminent desire dripping like honey.

His lips curl into a Cheshire grin, revealing his teeth and reminding me of the monster beneath—*my monster*. "I'll be anything you want, Nicolette. Whether it's magnificent, deranged, spectacular, or a fucking fiend. It's all for *you*."

He drags himself back onto the bed as one of his shadows curls around and gently lifts my leg, offering it to him. He takes it delicately in his hands, running a claw down the inside to my knee, following it with soft kisses, his lips sending a jolt to my sensitive center with every touch. He drags his tongue from my ankle to my knee, sending a wave of heat over me. Lowering my leg, he settles himself between them, looking over my body with hungry eyes.

His knuckles caress my center as he licks the remnants of my orgasm from his lips. "I'm going to take you, little vixen. Finally, claim you in this realm and not just in your dreams. And I'm going to draw it out for as long as I can. I want you to remember this night for the rest of our immortal lives."

I don't think he realizes that I will remember every instance his large, powerful hands have touched me, every heated glance he's sent my way, and every wave of pleasure he's sent crashing over me. He has consumed me in every way, and finally being claimed by him—as *his*—will become a part of who I am forever. It will override every version of myself, both good and bad, and shape me into exactly who I'm meant to be.

His.

Kryx's thick cock pushes at my entrance, and we moan in unison. "You're so fucking wet for me," he says roughly. He moves in closer, taking me inch by agonizing inch, his piercings sliding against my inner walls, hitting my G-spot and making me see stars. "*Dripping.*"

"Oh, God," I cry out as he takes me to the hilt, his cock filling me and his shadow filling my ass. He holds still for a moment before slowly pulling back out, my inner walls clenching around him, begging him to stay.

He lowers his face, his expression borderline terrifying, his hand still gripping my throat and pressing his nose to mine. "Do you not remember what I told you? *I* am your god now. Your fucking *devil*," he growls. "And you, little vixen, are my salvation. My *damnation.*"

I wrap my hands around his horns as he finds his rhythm, taking his sweet time with me. "Kryx, please," I pant, pushing my feet into the mattress, grinding into him and putting some relief to my sensitive clit, but his shadows force me back down, holding me in place.

He picks up the pace, driving his cock right into my needy cunt, his piercings continuing to hit my G-spot. My entire body tingles as the fire crackles wildly at our backs, the storm outside nothing like the one in here as Kryx finally claims me as his mate.

CHAPTER 16

Kryx

My cum drips from between her legs, soaking the sheets beneath her. I drag my fingers up her center and push them inside her, not letting another drop go to waste. "So fucking beautiful," I whisper. "And all fucking *mine.*"

Her eyes brighten at the sentiment, her lips curling into a mischievous grin. "Is that all you've got, Krampus?"

Little fucking brat.

I growl as I flip her onto her stomach and yank her toward me, her ass in the air. My shadows grip her wrists and bind them tightly behind her back. "What a brave little vixen, taunting the demon of Christmas."

I grip her hips as I line my cock up with her ass, letting a stream of spit cascade from my tongue, coating her tight hole. She gasps, her fingers curling into fists as my claws anchor me as I take my sweet time filling her with my cock.

"Kryx," she gasps. "Oh, oh, *fuck.*"

My piercings vanish one by one as I chuckle darkly. "I'm claiming all of you, little vixen. Filling every hole with my cum from now until the end of eternity. I was gentle before, but now I'm not holding back."

I slide into her as she chokes out a moaning scream. I reach down and grip her bound arms, lifting her and slamming into her tight ass. Every inch of her was made for me, our bodies merging into one, dripping with desire.

My balls tighten, and a sharp tingle climbs up my spine. I growl, sinking my teeth into the crook of her neck and leaving another mark to remind her of who she belongs to every time she looks in the mirror. She screams my name, and I come with a valiant roar, my feral side taking over, nearly causing me to blackout as I take her over and over again, barely noticing the sun rising in the dark sky, only to set again.

Nicolette and I have been fucking for nearly two days, solidifying our mating bond. I've been searching for this missing part of myself for centuries, and now it's finally clicking into place, making me feel more powerful than ever. Her defiant strength adds fuel to my fire. And as much as I want to stay in that cabin, taking every part of her until we burn up and become nothing more than ash in the snow, I have a duty—one I can't ignore any longer.

I've reluctantly left her side, but she is safe, warm, and satiated in her bed, the fire burning brightly as another snowstorm relentlessly approaches. I glance over my shoulder through the cracked bedroom door for one last look at her sleeping form, her chest rising and falling as she drifts deeper into the dreamscape I've created for her.

I glance back at the fire, concentrating on the flames as they lick the side of the hearth before bursting wide open. I step through the portal, my hooves sinking into the thick snow of the North Pole, rising above my ankles. Nick's castle looms in the distance, blending into the gloomy, arctic landscape, surrounded by storm clouds.

A growl rumbles from behind me, the sound muted by the fierce winds that would tear through any mortal. I feel the smooth grip of my whip as it materializes in my hand, my fingers tightening around it as I turn, coming face to face with one of Nick's horrific reindeer.

It's one of his lesser-known spares, not a beast from the Christmas songs children sing, but it's just as dangerous. Its eyes burn like hellfire, and its sharp, jagged teeth flash from its maw as its mass of antlers curls around its head in every direction, ready to impale its next victim.

Flicking my wrist, I crack my whip into the air, just inches from its revolting face. It rears back, letting out a squealing scream that cuts through the air, caught by the wind and swirling past me. I crack my whip again, the long, sharp tendril wrapping around its antler, the barb scraping its skin. I pull it down to the ground, smashing its face into the crisp, white snow.

The beast throws its head, jerking me forward and causing me to stumble and land on my knees, with the icy snow sticking to my fur. Thunder claps in the distance as the beast gets back on its sharp hooves, dragging me face down through the snow. Another screeching cry rings out, along with another crash of thunder that shakes the ground. But it's not thunder—it's the sound of antlers clashing as two more reindeer approach, their racks locking as they swing their heads in warning.

"Fuck," I breathe, because these monsters are the last thing I need to be fighting and wasting precious time that I could be spending with my mate. The smell of death and decay fills my nose as they circle me, their maws dripping with blood and gore —at the ready for a chance to bore me with their antlers.

I push myself up, rising to my knees as my whip is ripped

from my grip. I breathe heavily, the cold burning my throat as I call on my chains. I stand, the cold metal of the links sliding through my palms as they turn into maces, the barbed balls swinging, ready to strike. I scan the trees, searching for more as my chances diminish in this fight of three against one.

The wind picks up, swirling the snow into my face, blinding me as the rancid fuckers take their shot. Pain lances through my side as burning horns impale me, lifting me and slamming me into the trunk of a thick pine, my ribs cracking from the impact.

I land in the snow, crimson spreading through it like rot. Rising to my feet, I stumble as hot blood pours from the wound. I heave in a breath, my lungs burning as I steady myself, still gripping one of my maces.

The reindeer close in on me, their steps muffled as the howling wind intensifies their growls and gnashing jaws. "You got lucky, you fucker," I growl, swinging my mace and nearly hitting one of their faces. It rears back as the other two keep closing in, trapping me against a tree trunk.

I see a flash in the trees behind them, but I can't afford the distraction. I may be a demon and heal quickly, but even I can be killed, especially by vicious hoofed creatures like these. Now that I have Nicolette—*my mate*—I have so much more to live for and refuse to let these fuckers take that away from me.

I roar, the sound shaking the snow off the branches around us, causing heaps to fall in front of them and block me from their attack. I summon another whip, seize the moment, and flick it, the tendril curling around one of their necks, the sharp tip slicing through its skin. I pull back with all my strength, slamming it to the ground, but before I can react, I'm struck from the other side.

White-hot pain surges through my body, my vision darkening as I'm thrown to the ground. I try to stand, but the pain is blinding, and my limbs give out. I attempt to roar as I roll onto my back, but only a squeak escapes my lungs as one of their grotesque faces lowers to mine, licking its lips and revealing its sharp, jagged teeth.

I hear the other two fighting over who will feast on my corpse after this one is finished, their screeches deafening as my vision begins to fade. I think of Nick and what will happen to him if I'm killed. Will our bargain end, or will my powers pass to another demon, taking my place?

I'll never know.

I push the image of him away and picture Nicolette, wishing she would be the last thing I see before I become nothing more than a meal for these monsters—their bellies my unmarked grave. My heart slows as my blood mixes with the snow around me, freezing in the arctic cold. I exhale Nicolette's name, my last call to her as I feel my soul's fire turn to embers, ready to be snuffed out by my final breath.

The wind and reindeer howl before the smell of decay fades away, replaced by a snow-white floral scent as my eyes flutter shut, and I'm met with Death as it intertwines its fingers with mine, leading me away from the cold and back to the fires of Hell.

CHAPTER 17

Nicolette

My eyes fly open as pain radiates through my body, piercing my lungs and dragging me from my deep slumber. I cry out in pain and curl into a tight ball, screaming for Kryx. I take a deep breath as reality crashes back in, the silence of the cabin wrapping around me like a weighted blanket.

Kryx isn't here.

He tucked me in and left to tend to people on his list, promising me he would return as soon as he could. Even as I begged him not to go, he was concerned that his absence might raise suspicions and draw attention to whoever had attempted to visit the cabin a few nights ago. He left me safe and warm in a dreamlike state where we continued to explore each other, learning more about ourselves and leaving me yearning for more.

But all the pleasure I was feeling has been replaced with a deep pain that continues to take my breath away, seeming to burn me from the inside out. I sit up and press my hand to my chest, trying to ease the burn that's singeing my lungs. I wipe the sleep from my eyes and look around, seeing that everything is exactly as it was before I faded into my dreams.

I slide off the bed, dragging the sheet with me and wrapping it around my naked body. My muscles ache, but I welcome the pain as a gift from Kryx and all he has given me these past few days—orgasm after orgasm, kink after kink, and every part of himself, finally making me feel whole for the first time in my life.

I take care of myself in the bathroom, checking over the newest bite mark in the crook of my neck, a twin to the one on my inner thigh, and see that it's rapidly healing into delicate red scars. I wrap myself in my warm robe and slippers, then step out into the living room, craving coffee and something to dull the pain. But as I cross the threshold, the warmth that filled the cabin is gone, replaced by a cold wind blowing through the now-open front door.

I halt my steps as I look at the outline of a man, his tall, slender body leaning against the door frame. His skin is pale white, his eyes icy blue, with stark-white hair tousled by the blizzard wind swirling around him. He's dressed in navy pants and brown fur-lined boots that reach mid-calf. His broad chest is bare, displaying a large snowflake tattoo in the center, as a fur-lined navy parka flutters around him.

"Hello, *Nicolette*," the man says, his voice icy, sending a shiver down my spine.

I bump back into the doorframe, reaching for the fire poker that leans against the wall inside my room. "Who the fuck are you?" I ask, gripping it tightly with my trembling hands and raising it between us.

He chuckles darkly, the sound swirling through the room as he straightens up to his full height. He's not as tall as Kryx, but he still looms over me, making me feel small. "Kryx has been a very, *very* busy demon, hasn't he?" He looks around the cabin, drawing a deep breath through his nose, and his eyes widen.

"The mingling scent of your desires is intoxicating. I can see why he's so infatuated with you."

My arms shake as I hold the poker, adrenaline rushing through my veins. "Who the fuck are you?" I ask again, narrowing my gaze. "And how do you know my name?" This has to be the person who tried to enter the cabin the other night, and he must have been waiting for Kryx to leave.

"I'm wounded that Kryx wouldn't tell his little pet about one of his oldest friends," he says, his eyes darkening. "I'm Jack Frost —and you, Nicolette Evergreen, are coming with me."

"I'm not going anywhere with you," I bite out, the words sharp as I try to make myself look stronger than I feel right now. "Kryx will fucking kill you for coming here again."

The man steps toward me, a devious smirk on his face, and I lift the poker higher, aiming the sharp tip at his throat as another gust of wind blows through the cabin. "You can come with me willingly or kicking and screaming; either way works for me," he says, his voice pelting against my skin like frozen rain. "I do *love* a challenge."

I scream into my mind, begging Kryx to come back, telling him I'm in danger, but it's radio silent on the other end. The warm feeling in my chest is nearly nonexistent, replaced by a bitter cold that makes my heart feel as though it's cracking like ice.

Where are you, Kryx? Why aren't you answering me?

Jack closes the distance and reaches out. I swing the poker at him, a fierce growl in my throat, but he catches it in his hand, the impact shuddering through me. In seconds, my hands are burning as the metal turns ice cold, frost searing into my palms. I scream in pain and let go, my skin tearing open as I stumble back and fall on my ass.

He twirls the poker like a baton as he straddles over my chest, a devilish smirk on his face. He crouches down, my body trembling with fear as his icy cold hands grip my jaw, forcing me to look into his arctic blue eyes. "What if I told you, human, that your fuck buddy is now nothing more than reindeer food?" My eyes widen as my chest feels as if it's caving in. "And that you're now mine for the taking?"

"You're *lying*." The words are choked, barely making it past my lips.

His face darkens, and his smile reveals his unnaturally white teeth as he lets out a chuckle that's icier than the blizzard winds rushing into the room. "I can't wait to show Nick his newest toy." He moves his face closer to mine, dragging his tongue up my jaw and nipping at my ear, making me shudder in disgust. "But be careful, Nicolette," he croons. "He loves to *break* his playthings."

My limbs ache as the cold seeps into them, making me unable to move. Frost coats my skin as the room flashes, the bright white blinding me as I'm ripped from the cabin and into the cold.

My body feels as though it's on fire, creating a stark contrast to the bitter cold that clings to my skin. I force my eyes open and take in my new surroundings. The ceiling is high, with large chandeliers hanging from the rafters, red wax dripping down the sides. I turn my head toward where a fire burns brightly in a massive fireplace, the mantle decorated with holly branches and candles.

My fingers twitch, brushing against the soft blanket beneath me. I lift onto my elbows, my head swimming as I take in more of the space. It's a bedroom, not the dungeon I was expecting to be thrown into. I'm in a four-poster bed with furs piled around me. I glance at the nightstand to see a golden, bejeweled goblet and a piece of fluffy, white bread that almost resembles angel food cake on a silver platter. I roll onto my side, reaching for it, and feel a tug at my ankle.

My eyes drop to the foot of the bed to see a braided leather rope tied to the bedpost that vanishes beneath the furs. I pull back the pelts and, horrified, realize I am no longer wearing my robe, but a red lace teddy that leaves nothing to the imagination. I swallow thickly, sensing something tighten around my neck. I reach up and touch the smooth leather of a collar. I attempt to remove it, but the buckle doesn't budge, and my fingertips start to burn before I jerk them away.

The latch of the large wooden door across the room clicks, and the hinges quietly creak as it opens. A woman in a short, red satin dress enters, holding a leather rope. Her stare is vacant as she moves toward the bed, her eyes unsettling as they fix on me.

"Where am I?" I ask, my words sharp as I yank my leg, trying to free my ankle.

The woman acts as if she didn't hear me as she raises the rope to my neck. I swat at her hand, causing it to fall and the metal clip to hit the stone floor with a thud. She bends over and picks it up, her face expressionless.

"Who are you?" I ask, but I am only met with silence and her vacant stare.

She reaches out and grabs the collar, yanking me forward as she clips the rope onto the O-ring, roughly tugging on it. I try to pull away, but the collar tightens around my neck, choking me until I stop struggling. She keeps a firm grip on the leash, unhooking my ankle from the bedpost and dragging me off the bed to my feet.

"*Stop!*" I scream. "Where are you taking me?!" But my shouts are lost on her and bounce off the stone, fading into the rafters. She doesn't even fucking flinch as I try to fight back. A dark chuckle echoes from the doorway, and I freeze, turning my head quickly in its direction, where Jack leans against the door-frame with a goblet in his hand.

He takes a casual sip, a criminal smile on his lips. He snaps his fingers, and the woman holding my leash turns to him. "I'll take it from here," he says in a voice that's slick as oil.

The woman leaves, but not before he takes the chance to tousle her hair and slap her ass, his eyes never leaving mine. "Nicolette." He whistles, inspecting me from head to toe. "My, my, how lovely you look all wrapped up in a bow." He winks as he steps into the room, closing the door behind him.

"Where the fuck are we?" I bark, taking a step away from him. "And where is Kryx?"

Taking another casual sip from his goblet, he makes a tsking noise. "Temper, temper."

"Tell me where the fuck we are, *right now*," I growl as I keep slowly backing away, the heat of the fire searing my skin as I close in on it.

He looks around, inspecting my room and appearing pleased with himself. "Why, Santa's Castle, of course."

My mouth drops open, and my heart pounds in my ears. "The North Pole?" I gasp, the collar squeezing tightly around my throat.

He grins, showing too many teeth as he places his drink on the table next to the hearth. "Nothing gets past you, does it, darling?" I blink, and suddenly he's on me, trapping me as he presses his hands on either side of my head, gripping the mantle. The fire's heat laps at my skin, threatening to turn the sheer fabric of the teddy into nothing but ash.

He leans in, running his nose along my jaw, inhaling deeply before pulling back with wide eyes as if he's seen a ghost. The look is gone as quickly as it appeared, his blue eyes darkening like a winter storm. He checks the leash hanging from my neck, moving his hand to run his fingers over the braided leather, curling them tightly around it. He yanks me forward, bringing me to his face, and licking his lips. I want to pull away from his icy gaze, but one wrong move and I'll fall into the fire—caught between two extremes with nowhere to run.

"What do you want?" I ask, trying to keep the wavering out of my voice, but I fail miserably.

He presses his nose against mine, tugging the leash up, forcing me to look at him. "To give Saint Nick himself a present and remind him who his favorite really is. It *is* almost Christmas, you know."

He steps away, the leash slipping through his fingers until he reaches the end, sliding his hand through the loop. I try to resist, but he overpowers me, dragging me like a dog behind him. "Please stop," I beg, but just like with Kryx's shadows, ice solidifies like shackles around my wrists and ankles, imprisoning me further. "Please." And at that, my lips are frozen shut, every cry for help muffled.

"Now, now, Nicolette," he croons, "we don't want to ruin the surprise for jolly ole Saint Nick, now do we?" He pulls me close, running his knuckles across my cheek. "He's going to have so much fun with you. I can't wait to see the twinkle in his eyes as he finds his pleasure, watching as he breaks you into a million pieces." He leans in, whispering in my ear, "It's my favorite part."

My eyes widen with fear, panic pulsing through me as Jack leads me through the castle. My bare feet ache with every step across the freezing floor, the pain like walking on glass. I look around and see sconces lighting the long hallway, their flames flickering across the walls, each decorated with mistletoe and holly. The tall tapestries start bright, depicting Christmas as we know it, stitched beautifully, but as we move down the hall, each scene darkens until we reach a large set of wooden doors that tower over us.

A deep laugh echoes from the other side, piercing the silence. Jack glances over his shoulder, his familiar devious grin spreading across his face as he pushes open the door and leads us inside.

The room is vast, with high ceilings and chandeliers hanging from the rafters, much like those in the room I woke up in. A long banquet table occupies the space, with a handsome, white-bearded man sitting at the head and a beautiful woman to his right.

"Jack!" the man exclaims, rising from his chair and nearly knocking it over. His eyes land on me, and I want nothing more than to cover myself as he surveys me, the twinkle in his eyes dimming as we near the end of the table.

"Nick. Clara," he says as he bows, "I brought you a present— a new *toy*."

The ice shackles bite into my skin as they both examine me. Clara's eyes widen as if she's seeing the ghost of Christmas past. "Where did you get her, Jack?" she asks coolly, her expression returning to neutral.

He shrugs. "Does it matter where I got her? She's for you." He throws his arms in the air. "Merry Christmas to all and to all a *good* night!"

Nick steps toward me as Jack grabs the back of my neck, forcing me forward. "Bow down to your new master," he says in a low, growling voice. "And keep your fucking mouth shut or I'll let him know you were Krampus's little whore." My lips part as he releases them from his magical hold.

My body trembles from both the cold and fear as Nick looks me over, inspecting every inch of me. He hooks a finger under my chin, tilting my face up to him. "What's your name?" he asks, his eyes narrowing.

My heart thunders, and my own name sticks in my throat, but I swallow hard and push it out. "Nic-Nicolette." I take a deep breath, the pain in my lungs easing with each breath. "Nicolette Evergreen."

Clara suddenly stands, her chair toppling backward,

exposing someone kneeling at her feet under the table. "Is this a fucking sick joke, Jack?" Her voice is sharp, aimed at his throat.

He stammers as she crosses the room, her delicate hand grabbing his neck, her fingers curling into his skin like claws. "Clara, I—" She tightens her grip, cutting off his words.

"You brought her into my home knowing full well—" she starts, but Nick raises a hand, silencing her, the air thick with tension.

"Evergreen," he whispers as he gazes into my eyes. His expression softens, and his hand gently lifts to cup my face as if he's holding the most fragile flower in his palm. He opens his mouth to speak, but suddenly the hall doors burst open with a deafening crash, filling the room with a roar, and causing the glass on the table to rattle.

I scream as Nick pulls me into his arms, seeming to shield me from the intruder as the voice bellows a single word.

A name.

"*Jack.*"

CHAPTER 18

Kryx

My skull throbs as I force my eyes open; the edges of my vision are blurred by the falling snow, making it hard to see. The air is filled with screeches and cries of agony from the reindeer until the sound of a blade slicing through flesh silences them, leaving only the howl of the wind.

A hand cups my face, tilting my head upward, and I'm met with black, voided eyes and long white hair that shimmers like icicles. I groan as I try to shift from my side, but they grip one of my horns, keeping me in place. "Fool," says a dark, feminine voice. "Fucking *idiot*."

I gasp for breath, one that burns my lungs. "It's good to see you too, Lussi," I wheeze.

She watches me, dark eyes flickering to bright amber. "You are lucky I found you when I did, Kryx." Her voice is light, yet dark—whole, yet hollow. "Or you'd be nothing more than a fresh meal for those beasts."

Lussi is more than a spirit of Christmas. Her abilities far exceed mine, as she can shift into anyone or anything she desires; her true form remains unknown to most—except for me.

Her eyes turn black again, her white hair flowing past her waist—a striking contrast to her flawless ebony skin. She lowers herself into the snow, unbothered by the crimson stain of my blood soaking into her white cloak.

She places her hands on my chest, her eyes widening as she pulls them back, surprise evident on her face. "*A mate?*" she says softly, as if it's a devastating secret. She looks around the forest, her gaze settling in the direction of Nick's castle. "Does anyone else know?"

"No, but I need to get back to her," I croak. "I've been gone too long already."

Her eyes flash, her face going blank as she shudders with a breath. In a blink, she's pulled back into reality. She turns toward the castle, then quickly spins her head back to me. "Someone knows," she whispers hurriedly, pressing her hands against my chest. "We need to hurry."

Warmth flows through me, heating me from the inside out as she heals my wounds. I gasp, drawing a deep breath as my lungs expand, stitching themselves back together. She rises, examining me before stepping back and extending her hand.

I slide my palm against hers, and she pulls me to my feet, running my other hand along my torso over the now-smooth, healed skin. Lussi watches me intently. "She is here, Kryx." Her voice is as dark as a storm cloud, her eyes swirling with emotion. "Ripped from her home by icy hands, eager to offer her to the Saint himself as a gift of good tidings."

I look at the castle, watching the storm approach, marked by only one person.

Jack.

My hands curl into fists. "I'll fucking kill him," I snarl. "And I will feast on his soul."

Lussi places her hand on my chest, her magic forcing me to

look at her. "You cannot kill him without it putting Nick at risk." Her eyes lighten, her irises shining like clear blue water before they revert to their inky black pools. "Your bargain with Nick is his bargain with Jack."

"Fuck." My nostrils flare, flames burning bright in my eyes, reflecting in Lussi's white hair. My mind reels, and my body burns to run to the castle—to Nicolette. "Then I'll take him within an inch of his life, remind him how easy he is to dispose of, and maybe Nick will just let him rot in a cell for all of eternity."

"Kryx." Her voice echoes in my mind, drowning out the chaos. "Ask the right questions of her when you arrive. Some skeletons are ready to come out of their closet."

My gaze shifts to the castle and then back to her, the wind blowing between us, stirring up the snow. "What questions?"

"She is your mate, *brother*, but that is not all she is in this world." The snow begins to spin faster, encircling her. "'Twas the night before," she says smoothly, and with a strong gust of frigid wind, she's gone.

I stare at the castle, and my vicious thoughts come crashing back, reigniting the fire burning in my chest. Jack will pay for laying a finger on what's mine and trying to take her from me. Just because I can't kill him doesn't mean I can't hurt him—lash him with my whips and chains. Throw him into the fire and watch him burn, only to drag him out, let him heal, and do it all over again for eternity.

My rage intensifies, and my breath turns to steam in the freezing temperatures. I grab my whip from the snow and communicate through my mind, desperately trying to warn my mate—to let her know that Krampus is coming to punish the person at the very top of my list, and to show her exactly how it's done.

I come crashing through the doors, Jack's name a roar that rips at my throat—the room shakes and the fire blazes out of the hearth.

The scene in front of me makes the whole room turn red as I see where Nicolette is standing, wearing nothing but lingerie, as if she's one of their fucking pets. I step into the room as Nick pushes her behind him. Clara's hand is around Jack's throat, her eyes widening as she takes me in.

"Kryx," Nick says, a hint of panic in his voice. "What are you doing here?"

My gaze shifts from Nick to Jack, whose eyes bulge from Clara's grip as he gasps for breath, before turning back to Nicolette. She's trembling, fear coursing through her, as she stares me down. "Taking back what's mine," I growl, letting the words resonate through the room.

Nick glances between Nicolette and me, furrowing his brow slightly. "*Yours?*"

Clara shoves Jack away, disgust clear on her face. "Get her the fuck out of *my* castle," she yells, the words dripping with disdain. "And *you*," she says, fixing her dark gaze on Jack. "I will deal with *you* later."

Nick turns toward Clara, his eyes wide with fury. "*Your* castle?" he snarls. "You don't call the shots here, Clara. This is my fucking castle. *My* fucking kingdom."

Her eyes burn as she lifts her chin defiantly, her human pet retreating further under the table and out of the line of fire. "Do you really believe that, Nicholas?" Her words drip like venom from a snake's fangs. "Or is that the lie that you tell yourself as you fuck your pets—fuck *me*—all while imagining them to be someone else?"

He crosses to Clara in a few strides, gripping her chin and forcing it upward. He stares down at her, the room heating as the fire in his eyes intensifies, igniting the evergreen sea within them. Tension thickens the air, vibrating between them as she narrows her gaze on him.

Nicolette wraps her arms around herself as her teeth chatter, and I'm on her in a few steps, my hooves loud on the stone floor —warning anyone trying to get in my way of her.

"Little vixen," I breathe, wrapping my arms around her and pulling her tight against my chest. She lets loose a sob, her body shaking in my arms. I kiss the top of her head, breathing in her scent, letting it fill my lungs and the deep hole in my chest. "I'm here. You're safe."

Out of the corner of my eye, Jack starts crawling across the floor toward the door. That bastard isn't going anywhere—not until I'm done with him. I raise my hand, a whip forming in my palm. With a flick of my wrist, a cracking sound slices through the tension as my whip coils tightly around his leg and drags him toward me. "Kryx, *wait*," he says like a plea. "I think there's been a misunderstanding."

My hand wraps around his throat, squeezing so tight that my veins bulge against my skin. Lifting him, I hold him at eye level, the toes of his boots scraping against the floor as he gasps for air. "You took what's *mine* and tried to give her away." My voice starts as a whisper, growing louder with each word. "You knew what you were doing the whole fucking time, and now, you're going to fucking *pay*."

His nails dig into my arms as he gags, his eyes pleading. "Y-you can't kill me," he wheezes.

I bring him close to my face, snapping at him and showing all my teeth. "I might not be able to kill you, Jack, but I can make you wish you were dead."

He stammers a response as Nick's voice cuts in, grabbing my attention. "Who the fuck is she?" he asks, his voice rising as his gaze shifts between Clara, Jack, and me, searching for an answer.

I open my mouth to answer him, but Clara cuts in. "You *really* don't know who she is, do you?" Her shoulders are squared, maintaining her air of power and elegance, but her words are almost... sad. If I listen closely, I can almost hear the quiet cracking of her heart.

"And *you* do?" Nick retorts, his words like a blade ready to cut her down.

Clara crosses the room to us, looking down her nose at Nicolette. I growl as she raises her hand, but she doesn't strike her; instead, she runs her hands down the red rivets of Nicolette's hair, cupping her jaw. Narrowing her eyes, she scans every inch of Nicolette's face, as if searching for something she lost long ago. "Do you know who you are and how you've found yourself here?" Her voice is low, the question only meant for Nicolette.

Nicolette steadies her breathing as I listen to the whirlwind of reasons she comes up with, running through scenarios but settling on Jack's revenge. And while that's the answer on her mind, it's not the one on her lips.

"Because I'm on the Naughty List," Nicolette says, shame thick in her voice. Clara tilts her head but stays silent, leaving the floor open for Nicolette to carry on. "Because I'm the daughter of a con artist, and I've used the same tactics he did to cut down unsuspecting yet deserving men at the knees. Tear their lives apart as I take them for all they're worth and carry on as if nothing happened."

Clara's face remains neutral, embodying the Queen of the North Pole. "And what about your mother? What role does she play in your life?" she asks, her voice icy.

Nicolette's brows furrow, and I see the pain flicker in her eyes, the image of her mother front and center in her mind. She clears her throat but still struggles to say the words. "She was the only good in the world—in my life."

Clara's neutral face cracks into a look of disgust. "She was no good, you *insolent* child," she seethes. "Nothing more than a harlot. A *whore*."

Nicolette pulls back, anger blazing in her eyes. "How dare you speak of her like that?" she snaps, her fists clenched at her sides.

Clara's eyes flick from Nicolette to me, her lips tightening before she shifts her attention back to Nick. "It's a shame you never got the chance to go back, isn't it? To give her the story-book ending you both so desperately wanted." Her words are cold as she looks at Nick, whose gaze shifts from her to Nicolette.

I drop Jack, letting his limp body hit the floor with a thud. "What are you fucking saying, Clara?" I grit out, pushing the words through my teeth, my lips curling into a snarl.

Her eyes flash, but she keeps them fixed on Nick. "That maybe, *Krampus*, the father she knows isn't her father after all, and that she's actually the spawn of another monster entirely."

CHAPTER 19

Nicolette

M y stomach lurches into my throat, threatening to spill across the floor as I stare at Nick—the infamous Santa Claus in person. Clara's words slam into me, piercing my chest and clawing out my heart. I examine Nick, noticing his piercing green eyes that sparkle in the light, the remnants of bright-red hair in his neatly trimmed beard, the color almost identical to mine.

Nick averts his gaze, his cheeks flushing as he barks out, "Get her a dressing robe. *Now*."

The servants standing at the far door, whom I've just now noticed, disappear behind it and come back moments later. A woman who can't be older than her mid-twenties with short brown hair approaches me, holding out a red velvet robe with white fur lining the collar; her dark brown eyes aren't as vacant as the woman who led me here, but she looks as if she's lost in a dream—flickering between sleep and reality. I reach for her, but before my fingers can touch the fabric, Kryx's clawed hands snatch it.

He gives the woman a sidelong glance as she backs away before turning on her heel and retreating to her station. As he approaches me, he holds the robe out so I can slide my arms in, letting it cover my shoulders. I pull it close and tie the sash tightly around my waist to make myself feel less exposed to these strangers.

Kryx stands behind me, his knuckles brushing against my spine and spreading warmth through my body. His gentle caress calms me, giving me the strength to step toward Nick, and I lift my chin.

He watches me, taking in every feature, his eyes softening with each second that passes. "You look so much like her," he says, his words barely above a whisper but resonating loudly in the deafening silence.

Kryx moves to my side, his arm slipping behind my back, his claws digging into the robe like an anchor. Heat radiates from him, hotter than the fire burning behind me. "What are you fucking talking about? What the fuck is going on here?" he growls, pulling me closer to his side.

"Tell him, Nick," Clara bites, her voice trembling with pain she attempts to mask with the venom she spits. "Tell them who you really are to her."

Nick turns and grips her by the throat, yanking her toward him. His cheeks flush from red to burgundy, the fire burning brighter in the hearth behind us. "What did you do, Clara?" His words come through his clenched teeth. "What did you fucking do?"

Clara juts out her chin as she reaches up and grabs him by the collar of his white button-down shirt. Her grip is tight as she demonstrates her own power. "Did you think I wouldn't know about her, Nick? That I wouldn't catch on to why you disappear throughout the year? That you would come home and seem to have no interest in our pets? In *me*?"

The last words are choked, but she clears her throat, straightens her spine, and maintains her composure. "Did you think I wouldn't know when she found herself pregnant? And when she gave birth to a child with twinkling green eyes and hair as red as holly berries?"

Kryx takes a shallow breath, and I glance at him. His eyes widen, and his mouth drops open. He steps in front of me, placing himself between us. "You manipulated the list, didn't you, Clara? *You're* the reason that Evelyn was on that list the same time every fucking year."

The Clauses' heads snap toward him, and for the first time tonight, Clara's eyes shine with fear. "And you did your part perfectly, *Krampus*." Her voice is smooth—a Queen addressing her wicked court. "You took care of the problem without anyone being the wiser, breaking that disgusting little toy apart piece by piece."

Nick's face pales as he glances between Kryx and Clara. "The list," he whispers, his head snapping back to Clara, tightening his grip on her throat. "You altered the fucking *list?*" The words thunder through the room, bouncing off the rafters and shaking the glasses on the table. "*How*, Clara? How did you fuck with the list?"

She claws at his wrists, fighting for the air he stole from her lungs as I take a tentative step forward, pulling my trembling body away from Kryx's grip. Their words soak into my skin like melted snow. I touch my hair, smoothing my hand over the red ringlets. I blink, fighting back tears as they sting my green eyes —replicas of his.

Everything I thought I knew about my life is a lie. But I don't know whether I should feel relieved or betrayed as I stand here, looking at the man who possibly gave me life and played a role in tearing it apart.

"*You're* my father. My *real* father," I rasp, interrupting their argument as I walk closer, square my shoulders, and look up at him, his massive body towering over me. But for the first time tonight, I don't feel fear—just a swirling mix of other emotions I can't keep up with. "And you let *her* destroy my mother."

He pushes Clara away, her body going limp and sprawling on the stone floor, gasping for air as she clutches her throat. He looks at me, his face seeming to age as his magic slips, revealing his mortal side.

He steps toward me, but Kryx positions himself between us. His teeth are bared as he grips his whip, ready to strike anyone who comes near me. "You need to explain yourself, Nick," he growls—ever the possessive mate.

Nick gestures toward the table. "Let's sit and—"

Kryx snaps the whip, the barbed tendril striking less than an inch from Nick's boot. "*Now*, Nick."

Nick scrubs his hand over his face, then slides it to the back of his neck. He walks himself to the table, grabs a goblet, and drinks it all in one go. Slamming it back down on the table, he yanks out a chair and lowers himself into it. Gripping the arms, he seems to be holding on for dear life as his eyes meet mine.

"Eve caught me one Christmas Eve as I was coming down the chimney," he begins, the words scraping against his throat. "She was sleeping on the couch next to the tree, and I wasn't expecting anyone to be there."

I don't speak as I take a seat across from him, filling my own goblet with wine and trying to drown myself in it. It's sweet, like sugarplums dancing across my tongue. I tilt my head back, nearly finishing it in one gulp. I stare into the goblet, half expecting it to refill itself with magic. After a moment, I finally look back at Nick, waiting for him to continue.

"It wasn't supposed to happen," he states. "I could feel her beating heart as it matched with mine, cracking my ice-cold soul like a warm spring morning." He looks at Kryx from where he stands behind me. "A part of me lit up like it never had before, and I couldn't stay away."

A door slams across the room, and we all turn to look at it, as Clara has left. She no longer wants to hear the man she loves confess his love for someone else, with Jack gone long ago.

"She never told me she was pregnant," he says with profound sorrow. "She only told me that I could no longer come around and that she had to end things, but I couldn't stand the thought of not seeing her. I came back week after week and watched as her belly rounded, ignoring the pull in my chest that nearly brought me to my knees."

He looks at me, his eyes now silver rimmed. "I would have never thought..." He trails off, lowering his face into his hands, shuddering in a breath.

"But why keep sending Kryx to punish her?" I ask, the answer already lingering in the air. "She's fallen ill and isn't herself anymore." My throat burns, tears pricking behind my eyes.

"If I had known..." He trails off again, quietly clearing his throat. "She should never have been on the list. I don't know how Clara did it, but it's clear that she found out about my... affair." His gaze shifts to Kryx. "She knew that you wouldn't be able to deny the list and would have no choice but to carry out her punishment. She's been altering the list for years."

My heart aches as the knot tightens in my chest, squeezing the air from my lungs. I have always wondered what caused her to decline so rapidly, to find herself losing her thoughts and living in a constant state of confusion. One of the things I have worked so hard for is a discreet way to pay for her in-home care so that she can stay in her own home. She made them move the bed to the living room, put the Christmas tree up year-round, with her eyes fixed on the fireplace.

I've tried to get her to move into an assisted living facility, where she could still maintain her independence but receive help from staff when needed. However, she refuses, saying that if she leaves the house, she'll never be found again. She has been telling me that for years, repeating it as a mantra when she starts to spiral.

It never made sense until this very moment.

"She's waiting for you." The words sound flat, and the knot in my chest keeps me hostage. "It's why she has refused to leave my childhood home and has moved her things to the living room. She's waiting for *you*." The last word bites, snapping at Nick's face as he jerks back in his seat.

"Your wife's scheme has driven her to madness. It eroded her mind, and the only thing keeping her here is her strong belief in you—believing you will come back to her." The knot in my chest begins to loosen, releasing a flood of emotions like a stampede.

"Kryx might have been the one doling out her punishments, but you're the one killing her. You have to fucking let her go, Nick." The words come out as a scream, hot tears falling down my face as my fists slam onto the tabletop. I stand, the chair scraping the floor beneath me, my chest heaving with every breath as a large hand gently grips my shoulder.

"He can't," Kryx says softly, a catch in his voice.

I turn, looking up at him as my face grows hot, rage bubbling beneath my skin. "And why the fuck not?"

Kryx's hands cup my chin, gently tilting it toward him. His face is stern, his eyes burning with an unending fire. "Because, little vixen, he is bound to her... through *you*."

"*Me?* What do I have to do with this?"

He looks at Nick, who stays slumped in his seat, hands covering his face like the coward he is. "They're connected through you—the child of two star-crossed lovers, binding their souls as one."

I shake my head and pull away from his grip. "Then be with her," I snap, turning toward Nick. "By being apart and leading her on, you're fucking killing her!"

"I can't," he breathes, his voice muffled from behind his hands.

"Yes, you fucking can, you selfish prick." The words pour from my lips, anger boiling over. "If you can bring other people here as playthings, then you can fucking bring her here as your soulmate instead of letting her suffer."

Nick raises his head, his mouth set in a grim line. But even his sharp, immortal features seem to dull, blur at the edges, and appear to age him as if he's human again.

Kryx wraps his arms around me, pulling me close to his chest. My back warms against him as he lowers his head, breathing me in. "He might be able to bring her here," he says into my hair, "but that won't save her."

"I don't understand." A sob wracks through me, making my body tremble. "Why? Why won't it save her?"

After his long silence, Nick finally speaks, his voice turning hoarse. "Because my bargain won't allow it, as my soul is already bound to Clara's for eternity. And even if we found a loophole, a way to make her whole again, Clara wouldn't let her live in the North Pole—let alone this castle."

My heart falls from my chest, splattering at my feet. My mother fell in love with a bargained soul, one she can never have, and despite that, she created me—a bastard child of a soulless demon and an angel on Earth. "There has to be a way," I sob, the words tearing through me as I drop my head into my hands. "There has to be a way to help her."

Kryx stiffens behind me, cold air brushing my back as he steps away. "Maybe there is," he says lowly. Without another word, he rips open a portal and steps through, watching as it quickly closes behind him, leaving me alone with the Saint—my *father*.

CHAPTER 20

Kryx

I step out of the portal onto a frozen ledge, my eyes following the hillside that slopes down into a valley. Small villages scatter across the land, their chimneys sending smoke swirling through the fierce winds. I stand at the entrance of a cave, its opening large but unwelcoming, serving to warn off unwary mountain climbers from plunging into the depths of Hell on Earth.

I casually step in, the archway shielding me from the harsh wind. My hooves click on the stone floor, echoing through the cavern as I follow the winding path. The veins in the stone glow blue, illuminating the way.

After what feels like forever, I come to a fork in the cavern, one path leading to my destination and the other to a maze from which no one has ever escaped. I follow the path I've only taken a few times, but I know it like the back of my hand. The walkway seems to tilt as I go deeper into the mountainside, with the floor warming beneath my feet.

A yellow glow shines through the cavern, acting as a beacon to my destination and letting me know that the only person who can fix this mess is home—waiting for me.

"*Welcome, brother,*" a euphoric voice says as it floats through my mind.

At the end of the walkway, an underground castle emerges from a vast cavern that descends straight into Hell.

Crossing the drawbridge, I enter the spacious, open entry hall. Tapestries from the past and scenes of the future adorn the walls, illuminated by sconces of blue flames burning brightly between them. A growl echoes through the hall, and I turn to face a great, white wolf. It stands at the bottom of a grand staircase carved from ice, its glowing yellow eyes shining as it bares its teeth in a snarl.

"Eira," I say, bowing before the wolf. "May I see my sister, please?"

The wolf huffs as she turns away, glancing toward the top of the stairs where Lussi stands, appearing as the formidable Witch of Winter.

"What brings you to my dwelling tonight, Kryx?" Her voice drifts through the air, sounding distant, yet also a whisper in my ear. "Twice in one day is considered too much by some."

I bow deeply while keeping my eyes on where Eira stands, careful not to allow her the opportunity to ambush me. Although Lussi and I are cut from the same cloth and considered equals in this world, she is an all-knowing being—what humans call a witch—yet she possesses power beyond what most could even imagine.

"I seek an answer, Lussi," I reply as I stand back up to my full height.

"You discovered the truth of your mate's heritage," she says as she descends the steps.

I take a deep breath. "Why didn't you tell me? Save me the trip back here?" I ask, even though I already know the answer.

"It was not mine to tell, but now that you know, we can speak freely of it." There's a ghost of a smile on her lips, and I can feel her joy as it ripples through the cavern, gently lapping against my skin.

Good. That's what I was hoping for.

"Her mother is losing herself, Lussi," I say, stepping a little closer, fully aware of Eira and her protective nature. "And I'm here to find a way to pull her out of the pit of despair that Nick has trapped her in."

Lussi steps off the last step, resting her hand on Eira's head and gently massaging the wolf's scalp. Eira leans into her touch, their bond stronger than anything I've ever seen. "And you suspect I know the answer, dear brother?"

I give her a slow nod as I clasp my hands behind my back. "Nicolette is my mate, and I have already claimed her as such; however, there is still a hole in my chest—a yearning I can't seem to overcome. I intended to complete the binding cere-mony with her before she was taken from me—before I knew of her lineage."

Lussi tilts her head, her brows furrowing slightly. "Does knowing her true lineage change how you feel about her, brother?"

My body lurches, as if her words punched me in the chest. "*Never,*" I bite, the word coming out harsher than I intended. Eira shows her teeth, warning me as I relax my shoulders and suppress my emotions. "Nothing could ever change how I feel about her, Lussi. I've longed for her for over a decade. And Nick being her father is nothing more than a fact to me, just a twisted branch on her family tree." I take another step, careful not to trigger Eira. "But her mother... she's suffering from Nick's infat-uation, claiming that she's his true soulmate—Nicolette, their star child."

Lussi only looks at me, her eyes shifting to mirror Nico-lette's bright green. "And you think you know how to save her?" she asks, cocking her head to the side, her curtain of stark-white hair falling over her shoulder.

Raking my teeth over my lower lip, I nod. "I believe there's a piece of Evelyn's soul with my mate that was given to her when she was born, since she couldn't give it to Nick. I came here to find out if there's a way, when I bind my soul with Nicolette's, to free it—to give it back to her mother." I stare into the imposturous eyes of my mate, pain pricking my chest at her absence, and hope that she's safe where I left her at the castle.

Lussi moves from the stairs toward a set of large, stone doors across the room, passing silently through them. Eira at her heels, staying between us as I follow them into a sitting room. Two plush velvet chairs sit in front of a blazing fireplace, with a bear skin rug at their feet. She takes a seat in one, relaxing back and casually crossing her legs.

Some consider Lussi to be the legend of the Snow Queen, and seeing her in such a regal pose, I might think her royalty as well. She gestures to the seat across from her as Eira lies at her feet. "Sit, brother. Conserve your energy."

I take my seat, but instead of relaxing back like her, I lean forward with my elbows on my knees. "Please," I rasp, the residual pain radiating through my chest from Nicolette makes it hard to breathe. I know I left her suddenly with Nick, but I don't believe he would allow anything to happen to her, especially knowing that she's his star child.

"It will not be easy, and it will hurt everyone involved during the process. And of course, there's always a risk." She watches the fire as if searching it for more answers. "Are you willing to take it, brother?"

My heart thunders as anxiety crawls across my skin. "What kind of risk?"

Her eyes shift, turning crimson, mirroring mine. "Of *death*."

The word hits me like a wave of arctic water, the shock nearly gagging me.

Death.

"I won't risk Nicolette," I growl, jumping to my feet. "I'm

doing this for her, but I will not lose her over a mortal—mother or not."

Eira rises swiftly to her feet, bares her teeth, and prepares to strike. Lussi raises her hand, and the tension in the room vanishes as she intervenes with her magic. "You will take the part of her that belongs to you, just as she will take the part of you that belongs to her. It's a fair exchange, one that must be made to complete each other, filling in all the missing pieces. Then, you will be bound as the fates have decreed."

I press my hand against my chest, feeling the pulse of my wildly beating heart. "But she has accepted me as her mate, and I claimed her as mine. Was that not enough?" I ask, lowering myself back into the seat, my claws curling into the armrests.

"For most beings, yes. But you were not created like most, and a demon like you—a Lord—must endure the extra steps to solidify your bond. However, these won't fix the issue with her mother." This time, it's she who leans forward. "For it to work, you will need to take her life and make her anew."

Take her life?

The air is sucked from my lungs. "*Kill her?* You want me to kill my mate?"

Even as the tension in the room rises, Lussi remains calm and at ease. "You will not be killing her, brother, but making her your equal. Such a position requires her to become a demon."

I stare into the fire, knowing that all Nicolette wants is for her mother to be free from this, and that she would be willing to do anything to make that happen. But the real question is, am I as willing? I finally have Nicolette, and for the first time in my eternally long life, I feel as though I have accomplished the most important task I've been assigned. I have found the other half of myself, but until she is free from this burden imposed on her by her parents, she can never be fully mine.

I turn back to Lussi, who casually sits in her chair, waiting patiently. "What do we need to do to achieve this, sister?" I ask, anxiety prickling my skin with a thousand needles. "And please, don't sugarcoat it or speak in riddles."

Lussi's face sharpens, her eyes darkening to pools of black. "It requires a sacrifice." My heart stops as she leans forward, her white hair appearing as if ink had been poured over her head, turning every strand coal black. She rises to her feet and offers me her hand. "And it can be no one other than her—the star child."

I stand in the snow outside the castle, replaying everything Lussi said and trying to figure out how to explain it to Nicolette. Ultimately, it's up to her how she wants to proceed. Her free will stops me from making decisions on her behalf, and even if I wanted to, it's still not mine to make.

I take a deep breath, letting the cold clear my lungs as I open a portal and transport myself back into the hall to face my mate and her father.

Nicolette jumps to her feet from where she sits at the banquet table. "Kryx," she exclaims, my name sounding like a prayer on her lips. She throws herself into my arms, burying her face in my chest. "Where did you go?"

Nick gets up from his seat, unsteady on his feet, a now-empty bottle of wine on the table in front of him. He stays quiet and only watches me through unfocused eyes. I look down at my mate, holding her close in my arms. "To find some answers, little vixen," I breathe. "To figure out how to fix what is broken."

I stare at Nick, wondering how we both ended up at the mercy of two Evergreen women—how we both allowed Clara to play her game for too long, seemingly unnoticed, without realizing the implications. Her own eyes, green with envy, reflected a love she would never have with Nick, even after she gave herself wholly to who she thought was her soulmate.

I don't blame Clara for her actions against him, but I do blame her for how she treated Evelyn and for manipulating me to carry out the punishments she wanted for her. Nick used his magic and charisma to lure her under the mistletoe and kept her there, slowly poisoning her until she was teetering on the edge of insanity. Still, it was Clara's actions that finally broke her.

Nick was selfish, and while he technically gave me my mate, he nearly destroyed her by letting her watch her own mother vanish, turning her into nothing more than a shell of herself.

I bring Nicolette's face to mine, slanting my mouth over hers and kissing her deeply, not caring who sees. Dragging my teeth across her bottom lip, I hook her chin between my finger and thumb. "I need you to listen to me, little vixen." I look to Nick with a fiery gaze. "I need you both to hear every word I say and heed every warning."

CHAPTER 21

Nicolette

The storm crashes into the castle, thunder booming and shaking the ground. I look at Kryx from where I sit on his lap, his arms holding me close. If anything goes wrong, if I doubt myself even a little, I could die or get lost in a dreamscape forever. This is much more than letting him claim me or giving him my soul; it's about giving him my entire life—every part of me.

My chest aches, and I tremble as he holds me in his arms, allowing waves of fear and dread to wash over me. I squeeze my eyes shut, trying to find a calm part of my mind—one I can escape to and ensure there is not a hint of doubt slipping in. *"Relax, little vixen,"* Kryx says into my mind, with each muscle relaxing as if his words touch every one.

He rises from his seat, scoops me up into his arms, and carries me to the bear skin rug in front of the fireplace. He gently lays me down on my back, the fire warming my skin. He then lowers himself next to me, curling his body against mine and brushing my hair away from my face.

He clenches his fist then opens his hand palm-up, revealing a small pile of shimmering sand. "Nicolette," he says softly, and my gaze shifts from his hand to his crimson eyes. "Come back to me in this world."

I nod. "I will. I promise."

He takes a deep breath, blowing it into his palm and scattering the sand across my face, where it settles over me. My eyelids grow heavy, and I immediately drift into my dreamscape.

The moonlight illuminates the clearing as brightly as a spotlight. In the center stands a four-poster bed, the spindles curling like intertwined trees. Beside it, Kryx stands with his hand outstretched, beckoning to me. A warm breeze brushes past me, lifting the skirt of my dress. The white linen glows brightly, reflecting the moon's ghostly light. I open my mouth to call his name, but my words are lost in the wind, carried away.

I stumble, and his strong arms catch me. I look up at him, seeing him exactly as he is. His pitch-black eyes shine with fiery irises, and his long, inky black hair flows past his shoulders. His onyx horns curl gracefully back on his head. I trace my fingers over the tattoos that cover his chest before running my hand down his gray skin, feeling each muscle flex under my touch. He's terrifying—a monster who literally haunts the dreams of his victims.

A nightmare.

My nightmare.

But my heart flutters at the sight of him. He's walked through centuries, searching for his other half while spending over a decade crossing into my dreams, waiting for me to finally come to my senses.

And I'm the one willing to risk it all.

He gently cups my face, fiercely pressing our lips together. The piercings on his lips bite into me as his tongue slides in, mingling with mine. He wraps his arms around me, pulling me back onto the bed, deepening the kiss.

His shadows curl around us, warding off any Nightmares

that might try to take hold as his hands glide over me. His claws shred the fabric of my gown to nothing but ribbons, the pieces fluttering away in the gentle breeze. I moan into his mouth as he cups my pussy, the sensation of him on my bare skin almost too much. I arch my back, pressing my breasts into his chest, my budding nipples aching from the friction between us.

"Kryx," I plead into his mouth as I reach between us and grip his hard length, his shadows slithering up, undoing his pants and pulling them from his body. His hard cock slides through my center, coating him in my dripping desire. I moan, the sound muffled as he swallows it down, digging my nails into his skin as his hand laces through my hair, roughly tugging at the roots.

I pant as he continues to thrust his cock between my folds, friction building over my aching clit, taking me higher. "*Come for me,*" he croons in my mind, tugging my hair harder as he sinks his teeth into the space between my neck and shoulder, reopening the scars that already dot my skin. I scream as the smell of my blood fills the air, the warm liquid staining my porcelain skin crimson. The pain sends me plummeting over the edge, and I come all over his cock before he even fills me.

"Such a good girl," he says aloud, lapping up my blood and healing the bite. "And as sweet as my favorite wine."

He rolls us over, laying me on my back as he positions himself over me. His shadows slide under my hips, pushing them up for him, letting my legs fall open. "So beautiful," he growls. "Eternally *mine.*"

He pushes into my pussy, taking me inch by inch, his piercings adding a hint of pain to the pleasure. "Kryx, oh... " He slides back out and slams into me, all the way to the hilt, forcing the breath from my lungs and bringing tears to my eyes.

His irises blaze with fire as he slides off the bed, still seated inside me as he drags me with him, stopping at the edge of the mattress. He grabs my ass, lifts me higher as he thrusts into me, going so deep that I start to feel lightheaded. My walls tighten around him as he finds his release, filling me with his cum, the warm liquid flowing down and pooling beneath me.

He remains seated inside me and gazes down, emotion swirling in his eyes. He leans forward, capturing my mouth in his as he runs his hand over my chest, placing his palm on my thundering heart. He pulls back, his eyes burning into mine with a look of resolve.

"This will hurt, little vixen," he says, his voice rough, his eyes becoming silver lined. "Please, forgive me."

"What will—"

My question cuts off as his clawed hand sinks into my skin, tearing through it, wrapping it around my heart—the one that only beats for him—and pulling it from my chest, and the world goes black.

I'm falling.

Fast.

The dark world around me is endless, and my screams are silenced before they leave my mouth. My chest burns, the fire consuming me, the smell of burning flesh filling my nostrils. I squeeze my eyes shut just as I hit the ground below, and I wait for the pain, but it never comes.

My eyes flutter open, and I find myself lying in a field, the moon shining bright above with a sprinkle of stars. I sit up, expecting to be back in my dreamscape, but this place feels different—this one isn't mine.

I stand, a deep ache in my chest making it hard to breathe, and look around, taking it all in. I'm in the middle of a valley, with a small stream flowing through the middle, and a waterfall on the other side feeding into it. The air is cool, like a late fall evening, with leafless tree branches scraping against each other, and the scent of decay and earth filling the air.

"Hello?" a voice calls—the sound of it immediately bringing me comfort and easing the burning pain in my chest. It's one I would know anywhere. "Is someone there?"

I turn and see a younger, more vibrant version of my mother. She stands in a fitted cream dress, her brown hair falling like autumn leaves down her chest and back. Her hazel eyes are bright, the moon bringing them to life as she approaches me.

"Mom," I choke out as she steps closer, holding out her hand. I take it as soon as it's within reach, pulling her into a warm embrace. "It's me, Nicolette," I say into her hair.

"Nikki," she says softly, like a lullaby. "Whatever are you doing here?"

The burning in my chest flares up, and I break free from her grip, instinct driving me to claw at my skin. The linen dress I was wearing before appears whole again, until I rip the bodice in an effort to stop the pain. My chest glows, the skin singing as a bright blue orb pushes through. I gasp as it escapes my body, leaving me feeling cold as I double over, pressing my palm against the hollowed space between my ribs.

I lift my head, my hair falling over my face, concealing the grimace that scrunches my features. My mother stands there, staring at the small flicker of flame as it approaches her—an ember caught in the breeze. "Nikki, what's happening?" she asks, reaching out until her fingers brush the flame, her hands wrapping around it as if she's a child catching a firefly. "What is this?"

She cups it in her hands, gazing down at the piece of her stolen soul and listening as it calls to her. She folds her fingers over it, clutching it to her chest. Her eyes widen as she takes me in, as if it's the first time she's truly seen me.

"Take it, Mom," I say breathlessly, my body trembling. "It's *yours*."

She looks between me and the ember, her lip trembling. "Nikki, what do you mean?"

"Please, take it," I whisper, my words turning sharp as the seeds of doubt begin to take root in my mind, and my human instincts threaten to take over—to *kill* me.

I look down and see my hands fading, becoming translucent. My mother stares in horror as she watches me start to vanish from existence. "Please, there's not much time. You deserve to live your life, Mom. You deserve to have the part of your soul that Nick took back and be whole again."

Her eyes widen, and her jaw loosens. "Nick?" She shakes her head, the flame flickering wildly in her hand. "*No*. It can't be."

She averts her gaze, her eyes turning silver rimmed, but before she can say another word, I force her hands against her chest, pressing the ember of her soul into her, giving her back the gift of her mind and her life—the missing piece.

My body fades faster as she drops to her knees, gasping. The dreamscape around me trembles; the trees nearby sway violently. "I love you, Mom," I choke, stepping back so she doesn't get caught in the crossfire.

I take another step, and my foot sinks into the earth beside the stream. I turn and see my reflection in the water as the ground stills. I recognize the face staring back at me, except for the eyes. Instead of green, they burn hot like flames, casting a crimson glow. I stumble back and gasp, squeezing them shut.

It can't be.

I turn to see my mother on her knees, still clutching her chest in disbelief. The faint glow of sunrise peeks through the trees as the pitch-black sky begins to brighten, the autumn landscape shifting to spring, the smell of rot fading away, replaced by the scent of strawberries and wildflowers. The mist of shadows dissipates, and the looming Nightmares vanish—evaporated by the infant sunlight.

There's a tug at my chest, pulling me toward the water, and I fight the urge to follow it just for one last glimpse of my mother, standing in awe at the changing landscape—becoming whole again. Her eyes meet mine, shining brightly, and I blow her a kiss. A searing-hot tear cascades down my face, landing in the stream below.

Steam rises from the water as I step into it, with the last thing I see being my mother's smile as she catches the invisible kiss that floats through the air and presses it to her cheek, just as the current pulls me under.

CHAPTER 22

Kryx

Her heart continues to beat in my palm as I am ripped from her dreamscape. Nick stares at it in horror, his hand over his mouth, muffling a choked scream. I did everything that Lussi told me to do—claim her body and then steal her heart. Her soul would tear at the seams, allowing her to send the pieces back to those it was stolen from.

I fall to my knees, pressing her heart against my chest as my claws pierce my skin, the air in my lungs freezing over, and the room tilting.

The fire in the hearth blazes, leaping out and ready to dance as I cup her heart delicately in my hands, where it beats like a war drum, calling her home from battle. The castle groans as the wind picks up, pulling the flames into the room as a portal opens nearby. Nick stumbles back as Nicolette steps through before it swiftly closes behind her, sealing off whoever was on the other side.

She's nearly translucent, her shiny red hair dulled, but her once-green eyes burn with fire, shining brightly. Her face is streaked with tears as she looks at me, her gaze falling to the heart I now clutch in my hands. She shifts her focus to Nick, placing her hand on her chest, with a soft blue glow illuminating between her fingers. She closes the gap between them, stopping less than an arm's length away.

"This is for you," she says lowly, her words devoid of emotion as she presses the ember of his battered soul to his chest. "Look at every memory and feel every emotion she ever had for you—the ones that drove her to madness. The ones she was willing to rip her own soul apart for. All for *you*."

She roughly shoves her hand against him, causing him to stumble back before falling to his knees and clutching his chest, crying out in pain. He releases sobs as a storm of emotions rages, raining down on him. I hold my ground, protecting the heart in my hands as the roaring wind subsides and the electricity in the air fizzles out.

Nick heaves a deep breath, coughing and choking as he remains on the floor. He looks up with a pained expression, but with each blink, it begins to fade. "Nicolette," he rasps, still clutching his chest. "Is she..."

"She's no longer yours," she says, her words ice cold. "Saint Nicholas is nothing more than a faded childhood fairytale—a vision that once sweetly danced in her head." His head drops as she turns away.

Her gaze drops to the bleeding heart in my hands, its faint pulse echoing through the room. "My heart belongs to you now," she says warmly. "It was always meant to be yours."

I stare at her, the knot in my chest tightening as tears prick behind my eyes. I fall to my knees before her and raise the heart as an offering. "And mine belongs to you, Nicolette. If you'll have it."

She stares at me, her eyes bright like the fires of Hell—like mine. "Kryx," she breathes. "What are you talking about? My heart is yours." She looks around as if I would leave something so precious lying on the ground, as if I wouldn't protect it with my life.

I hold my heart in my hand and tap my chest with the other. "My heart is yours, and yours is mine. We beat for each other until the end of eternity, little vixen. Two halves that will make us whole."

She falls to her knees and extends her trembling hands. I carefully place her heart into her awaiting palms as if it were a delicate baby bird. A cool breeze flutters through the room, and her eyes widen, as if she's just been let in on a secret. Gradually, she raises her hands to her chest, pressing my heart against it.

She gasps as a light, like a falling star, flashes between us. The heart that was once mine no longer sits in her hands but beats wildly against her ribs, echoing as it settles into her. She keeps her hands pressed to her chest as if she's afraid it will escape. With every beat, her firelit eyes burn brighter, her body solidifying again, no longer on the brink of disappearing forever.

I wrap my arms around her, pulling her close. Her head rests against my chest, listening as our hearts beat in tandem—for one another. My body thrums, and my veins heat up as the fire pulses through them. Nicolette sacrificed her soul and gave her heart to the Demon of Christmas, becoming one herself.

She looks up at me, a smile pulling up the corners of her lips as her cheeks turn rosy. "Are you alright?" I ask, cupping her face in my hand and tilting it up further.

"I'm better than I've ever been," she replies, her voice carrying a warmth I've never heard. "I've never felt this free."

"This is everything I ever dreamed of, little vixen—in your dreamscape and mine," I say as I kiss her forehead, breathing in her new scent of embers and vanilla.

She lets out a stifled laugh, emotion swirling in her once-sharp green eyes, now alight with a fiery glow. She gently holds my face and pulls it toward hers, her lips softly pressing into mine. "Mate," she whispers, the sound sweeter than any song. "My very heart."

I smile, feeling the urge to sink my teeth into her sweet flesh, causing my jaws to ache. That is, until Nick's boots scuff against the floor as he stands. We turn to face him, his skin pale as he keeps clutching his chest, the glow finally faded, leaving his skin unmarred.

"I really did love her," he says quietly, his voice pained as Nicolette stands, squaring her shoulders and looking him over with her molten eyes. "And I hope in time, you can forgive me for the agony I caused her. I was naive to believe that my choices didn't have any consequences for her and that we would be nothing more than two ships passing in the night."

Nicolette considers his words, giving him a nod. "My mother is whole again. Now it's time for you to fix what you broke with Clara. She deserves your half-assed apologies more than I do. Even if she did put my mother through Hell, two women shouldn't have to suffer because of the actions of one pathetic man."

She turns and opens a portal, glances back at me, then steps through, holding it open just long enough for me to follow her to her cabin in the woods, leaving Nick all alone.

We stand in her living room, the golden-hour light filtering through the curtains, illuminating the room brightly and making her glow even brighter. She looks like an eternal flame with her red hair and bright ember eyes, my heart pounding wildly in her presence.

She scans the room, noting the pile of snow at the front door left open by Jack and the fire still burning in the hearth. She lets out an exasperated sigh, her gaze flicking to mine. "Where do we go from here?" she asks. "Or are we to be condemned to a cabin in the woods forever?"

I chuckle. "Only if you want to, but I have a home of my own... a castle, actually."

Her eyes widen. "An entire fucking castle? And we've been here the whole time?" She gestures around the small cabin, frustration apparent on her face. "You've been holding out on me, Kryx," she says with a giggle, playfully swatting at my arm.

I can't help the laugh that escapes from my lips. "It's at the North Pole, but it's far enough away from Nick and Clara that they don't bother to visit, and I highly doubt they ever will now."

She looks around. "I'll miss this place," she says quietly, running her hand along the back of the couch. "But maybe it's time to let it go."

"Little vixen," I say as she turns toward me, leaning in and wrapping her arms around my waist, pressing her cheek to my chest, "we can keep it for you. It doesn't have to go anywhere. Use it as an escape when the North Pole becomes too dreary, and you want to feel the sun on your face. Experience the other seasons." I tilt her face up and lean down, nipping at her ear. "Another place we can fuck."

She plants her hands on my chest, playfully shoving me away. "You *naughty* demon," she says with a chuckle as her eyes catch the pile of snow again. "But what about Jack Frost? What will happen to him?"

The mention of Jack softens my hardening cock, and I exhale sharply. "I believe he will face serious consequences from Nick, and Clara will probably suffer as well." I brush my knuckles across her cheek. "But you are his daughter and my mate, so if you want to harden the punishment, I'm sure he will listen."

She shakes her head. "As fucked as it is to say, if it weren't for his act of adultery and her act of envy, I wouldn't be here... with *you*."

As fucked as it is, she's right. Fate knew what it was doing in bringing a demon like me—one who was born to inflict pain and suffering on the naughtiest humans—to someone like Nicolette, whose heart was almost as dark.

"Why are you looking at me like that?" She cocks her head to the side, studying my face.

My chest pounds as my primal side presses against my skin, making my mouth water as my desire for her takes hold. "Your heart burns for me," I say roughly. "An eternal flame in my chest." I rest my palm over the thundering heart that rattles her ribs. "But that's not the only thing that's heating. And now that you are a demon queen, I want your blood and your cum on my tongue, to see if they're both still just as sweet."

Her eyes blaze, flames matching mine as she backs toward the front door, my instincts on high as I track her every move. "You'll have to catch me first." She flashes a devious smile and turns, her legs carrying her out the door and dashing through the snow—sending a wild thrill through me as I give her a head start.

CHAPTER 23

Nicolette

"Oh, little vixen," Kryx calls, sounding as sly as a winter fox as I dodge between the trees, the demon hot on my heels. My cotton dress flies behind me, catching on branches and thorns, tearing from the hem up. His heartbeat pounds in my chest as he chases me, the thrill sending a pulse straight to my clit.

I leap over the frozen river, my foot slipping on the ice, causing me to fall to my knees as the cold sinks its frigid teeth into my skin. I scramble back to my feet, only to be shoved down again, a burning hot hand pressing between my shoulder blades. "Now, now," Kryx says with a tsk. "Did you really think you could get away from me so easily?"

His hand grips my hair, yanking my head back as his tongue traces up the side of my throat, nipping at my ear. I try to speak, but all I can manage is a low moan as his knee slides between my legs, pressing against my center, and I grind against him.

My skin heats, melting the snow around us and causing it to drip toward the frozen river at our feet. Kryx's shadows slip beneath my hips, lifting my ass as I hear the laces of his pants pulling free, his cock already pressing against my entrance.

His body cages mine, his scent of pine and smoky embers filling my nose as he teases me with the head of his dripping cock. "Fuck me, Krampus," I purr. "Fuck me like the naughty demon lord you are."

He slams into me with a growl, his piercings sliding over my G-spot and making me see exploding stars. His hand slips away from my hair, curling around and pressing against my throat, causing my eyes to roll back. His thrusts become erratic before he emits a vicious roar, shaking the trees and warning everything nearby to steer clear of the monster.

Suddenly, he flips me onto my back, spreading my legs wide as he consumes my pussy, his tongue spearing into me as his teeth gently graze my pulsing clit. "*Yes,*" I moan, gasping for air as fiery warmth spreads through my abdomen, with wave after wave of my orgasm crashing over me—drowning me.

Will he someday get tired of this? The question comes out of nowhere as he drags the tips of his claws across my ass, making my skin sting.

Kryx lifts his head from between my legs, his face smeared with a mix of our cum, sporting a sinister smile. "I will *never* tire of you, little vixen," he says, licking his lips. "And don't you ever have such a thought again, or you will be punished for the rest of eternity."

"Is that a threat or a promise?" I tease breathlessly with a fiery grin on my lips.

"It's always a promise, but I can make it whatever you want," he purrs as he climbs up my body, pressing his lips to mine and forcing his tongue into my mouth, coating it with our desire. I get lost in his kiss, his touch turning tender as he slides his hand to my nape, not letting me go.

"*I love you, little vixen,*" he says into my mind. "*Our love was written in the cosmos, singed into the earth by the fires of Hell, and so long as I'm breathing, it will never burn out.*"

Kryx altered my entire life and gave me a new one. He

revealed secrets and gave me the power to free my mother's lost soul. He's a demon, but he's nothing like the bedtime stories told of him. He's cruel, but also merciful. Domineering yet submissive. A vicious nightmare, but a dream come true.

And he's mine.

My heart.

My soul.

My *mate*.

He slowly pulls back from his kiss, his lips sliding across my jaw and down the curve of my throat, his body merging with mine. I'm lost in him, feeling his claws scrape across my mind, my legs entangling with his. The wind whirls wildly around us, the icy branches cracking, and the flutter of winter birds circling us fills the air. I should be worried about what is lurking in the shadows, watching us between the trees, but I'm with the scariest thing this forest has ever seen, and I've never felt safer—more secure.

I slide my fingers into his hair, gliding them up and down his horns, his cock hardening again as he slides it between my folds. *"And I love you, Krampus,"* I say, letting him feel the smile on my lips as they press into his. *"My heart is yours. For eternity and long after."*

I feel dust brushing against my face, sprinkling into my eyes, and the world around us begins to fade, darkness draping over us like my favorite quilt. I feel the earth shift before we're slowly lowered into a dreamscape. I open my eyes, expecting the clearing that has become my second home, but instead, I'm surrounded by walls of ice, blue veins glowing from beneath them, filling the cavern with their light.

"Kryx," I say out loud. "Where are we?"

His hand cups the back of my head, a gentle smile tugging at the corners of his mouth. "I know all your dreams and desires, your darkest secrets. You have not only sacrificed your soul but also given me your heart." He presses a soft kiss to the corner of my eye, nuzzling his face into the crook of my neck. "And now, I want to show you more of me, starting with my own dreamscape."

He pulls away, rising to his knees as he offers a hand to help me sit up. I look around, taking in the winter wonderland around us. It's filled with snow-dusted evergreens, lights twinkling among the branches like fallen stars. Holly bushes dot the clearing, with mistletoe growing wild through them, and the scent of pine fills the air. In the center stands a large four-poster bed with tall, pine spindles, draped with sheer fabric that flows down and pools on the ground.

The duvet is bright white, gently spread over dark green silk sheets, with a mountain of pillows of various shapes, colors, and fabrics piled in front of the headboard. A massive stone hearth rises from the snow-covered ground, a fire crackling inside, with embers floating like fireflies in the air, warming the entire clearing.

"Kryx," I breathe, my breath clouding in front of my lips. "This is *beautiful*."

We rise to our feet and walk over to the bed, his shadows pulling back the duvet as he guides me onto the mattress, sliding in beside me. He lowers me back, and I gasp at the vastness of the stars above us, constellations twinkling like lights on a Christmas tree. He chuckles, cupping my cheek and turning my face, softly pressing his lips to mine.

"I made it into the wonderland that I dreamed of living in with you," he says, his voice smooth. "I saw what your dreamscape used to be, and I always imagined I'd be able to create it for you again and make up for all the pain and suffering I caused."

I curl into his side, letting my fingers drift over his chest, swirling one around his pierced nipple, where I hear him quietly gasp. "You were just doing your job; the blame falls on the Clauses. But I don't remember asking you to stop inflicting pain on me," I say, sliding my leg over his hips and rising to straddle him. "In fact, I think it's time *I* return the favor, *Krampus*."

His grin sharpens, and his eyes flash with fire as a pile of chains appears beside us on the bed, softly clinking, with a flogger resting on top. He runs his hands up my thighs, gently scraping the back of his claws and sending a shiver up my spine while heat curls tightly in my lower abdomen. "Sticks and stones may break bones," he says lowly. "But whips and chains excite me, little vixen. Make me *suffer*." He gives me a wink and licks his lips.

I grin as I reach over and grip the flogger, sliding the leather tendrils across his abs, watching as the dense muscles flex tightly. "You've been a naughty demon the last decade," I say with a flick of my wrist, the flogger cracking across his skin. He moans, his claws digging into me just as shadows curl around his wrists, lifting his arms above his head. "And your eternal punishment begins tonight."

He yanks on the shadows, his eyes wide with surprise, realizing that I've manifested my own, guiding them with my silent commands. His hair is fanned out on the red satin pillow beneath his head, his eyes burning bright as he scrapes his teeth across his bottom lip. "Oh, my little vixen has learned a new trick," he croons. "How *delightful*."

I drag the flogger across his chest, flicking my wrist and causing a hiss from between his sharp teeth as the leather bites into him. "It's not the only thing I have up my sleeve," I say, my voice going husky as snow begins to fall around us, the flakes kissing our cheeks.

"Dash away, little vixen," he breathes as I grind my center onto his cock. "Put yourself back at the top of the Naughty List."

Oh, Krampus, I fully intend to.

Our moans fill the clearing as our hearts beat as one, burning as brightly as an open fire. I have found my home, but not in my cabin or his castle—in him. He is everyone's nightmare, but my dream come true, and I never want to wake up.

I, Nicolette Evergreen, have been called every name imaginable except for nice. I used to be a thief, a fraud, and a con artist. But now, you'd better watch out because, thanks to the demon of Christmas, I can be much, much worse.

For someone like me, it's a pain to be nice, but oh, what fun it is to be *naughty*.

EPILOGUE

Kryx

'Twas the night before Christmas, and all through the castle, not a creature was stirring, except for my mate, as I woke her from her slumber with my cock, feeling her walls tighten around me as she let out a somnolent moan. I wrap my arms around her naked body, gently cupping her throat and pressing her against my chest, my fingers swirling over her swollen clit.

"Kryx," she moans, her mane of curls wild as she presses her head back, her sweet scent wafting into the air. "You're a fucking bastard."

I chuckle as I bite into the crook of her neck, my teeth sinking into her skin, once again marking her as mine and making her come before she even opens her eyes. Her moans shift to sharp pants and whimpers as I take my time, letting my piercings tease her G-spot and keeping her on edge. Her nails dig into my arms as her hips buck back, and I tighten my hold on her as that familiar tingle races up my spine.

I slam my cock into her, growling as I fill her needy cunt with my cum, not letting a drop escape as I press deeper into her. She grinds her hips against me, clenching her inner walls as she reaches behind her, gripping my nape. "You are far from finished," she rasps as her nails scratch the back of my neck.

"I didn't intend for you to wake from your slumber so soon," I say cunningly, nipping at her ear. "I need to use more of my magic on you now that you're my demon queen."

I turn her onto her stomach and gently pull out, our mixed cum dripping and sliding down her inner thighs like a work of art. I lower myself, running my tongue from her cunt to her ass, smearing our desire across her skin and tasting us as I grip her hips. Her arms are outstretched, her fingers gripping the sheets as I devour her from behind. Her body heats as she presses her face into the pillow, her screams of pleasure causing the down feathers beneath the silk case to flutter.

We've been like this for days, locked inside my castle, showing her my side of the North Pole and only slipping away when my duties as Krampus call, but not before sending her to one of our dreamscapes. When she's awake, she has been exploring every part of her new home, from the vast library to the lurid dungeons below, where I took the opportunity to shackle her to the wall and show her *exactly* how I punish my prisoners—though she seemed to enjoy her punishment much more than they ever did.

Naughty girl.

She befriends the ice giants who guard the gates, along with the snow fairies that take care of the castle, mimicking the jobs of the humans that Nick steals, but with much better working conditions. She has fit right into life in this desolate land, bringing warmth and light to this drafty castle, all of which my faithful servants seem to be enjoying.

She's not as frightful as she makes herself out to be.

Her cabin in the woods has been concealed from humans, protected by wards that cause them to unknowingly avoid it, allowing her a place to bask in the sun when the seasons change in the lower lands. It's also a safe place to bring her mother, whom she has been looking forward to seeing tomorrow, on Christmas Day.

Evelyn doesn't remember her time with Nick or the pain she endured due to Clara's intense jealousy, which is for the best. However, she is aware that he's Nicolette's father and that Krampus is her mate, which I showed her through a dream. I could glamour myself into a human form, but it was easier to bind her to secrecy and reveal Nicolette's new life gradually. Evelyn has been living worry-free, as we ensure she has everything she needs, and she continues to reside in Nicolette's childhood home.

"Kryx," she growls. "Do *not* think of my mother while you're inside of me. She will have your full attention tomorrow, but tonight, I'm all you should be thinking of."

I chuckle, purring as I spread her legs, forgetting that she can now wander into my mind, just as I can into hers. "Apologies, little vixen," I whisper softly as I kiss her inner thigh. "I'm looking forward to the feast tomorrow with your mother, but tonight, I plan to feast solely on you."

We're in the honeymoon phase of our mating bond, which can take centuries to settle, and I plan to make the most of every moment. I might have been the one born a demon, but she is just as wild as I am. Her transformation has only made her naughtier, and while she's been behaving herself, I don't think it will be long before she insists on coming with me to enact a punishment.

And when that day arrives, I'll be as giddy as a kid on Christmas.

I pull away and climb up the bed, lying on my back next to her. She whimpers in disappointment until my shadows curl around her waist, lifting her and prompting her to sit on my face, where I spear my tongue into her cunt and continue my feast as I slap her ass. She grips my horns, gliding her palms over them, stroking them like my twitching cock.

I feel the cool sensation of shadows on my wrists as they twist around and pull my arms down, pinning them to the bed while she continues to ride my face. She's ensnared me in her web of shadows, taking from me just as I took from her for a decade. And there's nothing I wouldn't give her.

So goddamn naughty, my little vixen.

She lifts herself and turns, settling back onto my face as her hands slide down my body and grip my shaft, a shadow pressing against my ass. "You're not the only one who gets to feast," she purrs, lowering her lips to my cock, flicking her tongue over the tip before swallowing me whole, her shadow plunging into me.

I snarl as I struggle to lift my arms, my fingers itching to touch her and play her like a fiddle, but the shadows hold me in place. *"Tell me that I belong to you, Nicolette,"* I beg into her mind while feasting on her dripping cunt, her spit coating me and sliding over my tightening balls as she works her naughty mouth up and down as her shadow fucks my ass. *"That I'm yours."*

"You belong to me, Kryx," she says, her tendrils brushing against my mind as she gags around my cock, her fingers gripping my thighs, her nails digging into my skin. *"And only me."* Her voice is low and husky, her desire dripping with every word as her cum trickles down my throat.

"Again," I plead, my pleasure building, setting my body on fire as we find our rhythm. *"Tell me again."* I could overtake her with my own shadows, feeling their presence as they wait around the bed, but this is like living a dream. I'm usually the one in charge, and I never thought I'd let anyone dominate me, but there's no one else I'd rather be at the mercy of than her.

"You are mine, Kryx," she croons, *"Your heart. Your body. Your cock. It's all mine."*

I growl, letting the vibrations flow through her, rumbling the room as she moans, doing the same to me. My vision blurs, ecstasy pumping through me as my cock jerks, my cum cascading down her throat as her own desire coats my face, pooling on my tongue and warming me like the sweetest of wines.

She rises, lifts herself away from my face, and spins around, straddling my chest. She runs her fingers across my lips and then brings them to hers, sucking them into her mouth and tasting herself—a queen on her throne.

"You are oh so naughty, little vixen," I say breathlessly, the shadows slowly releasing my wrists, allowing me to run my hands up her body, palming her breasts, and playing with her nipples. "And it's the only list you'll ever be on."

She lowers herself, where I capture her nipple between my teeth, and she lets out a gasp, my hands roaming over her curves, and settling on her hips as I glide my still-hard cock between her folds. "Merry Christmas, Krampus," she says as she lowers her face and brushes her lips over mine.

"And to a very *naughty* night," I reply with a twinkle in my eyes, wrapping my arms around the only gift I've ever wanted as my shadows tie her up with a bow.